Table of Contents

Pennies From Hell

"**M**r. Kenneth. Come quickly!" my crew chief Ahmet yelled up to me. "We've found something!" He was standing in a deep pit that the workers had been digging into the side of a small plateau. They had spent the entire morning using a rusted yellow excavator to remove a huge boulder and haul it away, uncovering dirt that had not seen the light of day for millennia.

I lowered my iPad, which had dozens of tabs open to architectural plans, and glared down at him. He was a thousand feet from where I was standing, but I could see this was something exciting. His invariably solemn demeanor had been replaced with wide-eyed anxiousness, his normally monotone voice elevated to a level of enthusiasm I didn't realize he possessed.

I sprang from the seat of my open-air Jeep and descended toward him on a quick jog, my interest piqued. If I'd known then what I know now, I would have fired up my ride, driven straight to the airport, and hopped onto the first flight out of Turkey.

As a civil engineer, I'd been working on a bridge project in the Urfa Province near the border with Syria. I'd left the windy city of Chicago a dozen years earlier to escape the cold, snow, and urban decay. The child in me always dreamed of exploring the exotic destinations I saw on TV. In fact, I got my degree so I could travel the world without joining the military. I could think of no better way to experience a little adventure while still making a decent living without getting shot at.

Qatar, Vietnam, the Philippines . . . My wife joked that I had more frequent flier miles than some airline pilots. I had done things that friends I grew up with could only fantasize about: petted a full-grown Bengal tiger, walked among the Great Pyramids at Giza, even drank the infamous Kopi luwak, a coffee made from beans that have been eaten and then defecated by Asian palm civets. I did it on a dare. It took several weeks to erase the imaginary injuries it did to my taste buds from my mind.

Our worksite was only twenty kilometers from Gobekli Tepe, a recently discovered archaeological marvel. It's the world's oldest religious shrine, though what gods they worshiped there is up for debate. Over 12,000 years of age, it makes the Sphinx seem like a baby lion cub, predating Stonehenge by a remarkable six thousand years.

I was enthralled by the temple's circular walls and massive megaliths. That was the main reason why I was so eager to accept this gig. I had been praying we would discover some kind of ancient artifact. The loosely connected society that erected the temple lived before humans knew how to make metal or pottery. A nomadic cluster of tribes united together to raise monoliths as tall as twenty feet and weighing over fifty tons, all before the wheel was invented. Then master sculptors embellished them with exquisitely designed foxes, vultures, scorpions, and other creatures.

How did these Neolithic people, barely more advanced than Neanderthals, create such divine carvings? They had not even begun farming, still lived by hunting and foraging, yet somehow, they had leapt light years ahead in their vision of architecture. The tinfoil hat group insisted that aliens from outer space had helped the Egyptians build the pyramids. If so, who helped these Stone Age prodigies construct this monument of such epic proportions? And why did the tribes who built it over centuries of grueling labor suddenly bury it and walk away? Merely a thousand years after erecting it, they covered the entire area in sand and debris and stripped the holy place from their memories. Did they want to preserve it from the ravages of nature's cruel elements, so it would be rediscovered by future generations? Or did they want to hide it, conceal it away from the rest of humanity for the remainder of time?

My steps slowed as I closed in, my shoes half burying themselves in the freshly harrowed soil. I stopped and gazed at a prehistoric relic that was embedded under the boulder. Had it been purposely hidden there? I would have thanked God just to find a simple carving tool. This was so much more. Yet I know now that no god worth praying to would ever unleash such a cursed thing upon the earth.

I had to squeeze my eyes shut several times to focus and make sure what I was seeing was actually there. A primeval wooden box, preserved over the ages by its massive tombstone. The lid was intricately carved with a panoramic scene, the unmistakable view of a comet or meteorite hurtling toward what appeared to be the Tektek Mountain range, just a few kilometers away.

For a moment the thrill of discovery stole my ability to breathe. Forgetting all the archeological protocols that I had studied religiously for just this type of event, I dropped to my knees and dug in with my fingers. I barely noticed the faint scent of sulfur or the ominous clouds blotting out the suns, which had beaten us down throughout the operation. A strong, cold wind blustered in from the north, even though the breeze had been warm, calm and from the southwest all morning.

I tore the box from its resting place, clumps of dirty dropping from the bottom as I raised it. At first glance, the chest looked to be perhaps a foot square and four inches deep, lashed shut with some type of animal hide, which had decayed beyond recognition. I barely heard the disturbed mumblings of my crew, their religious beliefs agitated by the artifact.

What was inside? Buried treasure never excited me. Rubies and emeralds were for capitalists, those sad people inflicted with such greed that they were never happy with what was truly important in life. I wanted to be known as a scholar who unraveled the secrets of early humanity. To prove all the pompous historians wrong, that our history was far older than anyone believed. My sins were envy and resentment. Here was my chance to make them eat their words or look like fools.

Before I could open the top casing, a burst of flame as hot as a blast furnace erupted from the very hole I had just lifted the relic from. A gaseous explosion, not simply orange but a multi-colored rainbow of searing red, blue, and violet. It engulfed poor Ahmet, who was so intrigued by the discovery that he had crowded me for a closer view. He stumbled away, screaming as if he had been scorched by hellfire.

That scent of sulfur was overwhelmed by the stench of sizzling flesh. The other crew members rushed to extinguish him, but after mere seconds, his body had been burned beyond recognition, practically to the bone. I could even see portions of charred femur and tibia through his pant legs as he dropped dead to the ground.

Many workers fled the scene in terror. A few fell violently ill, projectile vomiting over the scene of the accident. One even winced as if shot in the gut. He spun to his knees, convulsing and coughing up blood. I stood like a statue, in total shock. I didn't feel anything—heat from the flame, sadness for Ahmet, not even fear of another eruption.

I kept my head while all others were losing theirs but only because the relic held me captive. I felt a vibrating power inside that made me tremble in primitive fear. I felt as if I had reverted into a man from that ancient era. My terror was as simple as it was obliterating. The force had stolen all modern logic and disdain for supernatural phobias from my thoughts and replaced them with the primordial emotions of a cave dweller.

I don't remember when or how, but at some point I must have snapped out of it and led myself back to my vehicle. I woke up in the middle of the night to the sound of policemen yelling and pounding on my hotel door.

I was in a blackout of mind-boggling proportions. Didn't know where I was at first. Barely knew who I was. I've never experienced a migraine, but my head was pounding from deep in the left hemisphere all the way down to my spinal cord. My throat was parched to the point that my tongue and the inside of my mouth was cracked and painful. My stomach felt withered, as if I hadn't eaten in weeks.

As I struggled to get out of bed, my entire body fought against me, stiff, sore, and not wanting to rise. I realized I had never even undressed, just covered myself with the freshly laundered comforter, muddy boots still on my feet.

I unlocked the door, and they nearly bowled me over as they entered. Five police officers—two lead investigators and three in uniform. They were gruff at first, angry that I had fled the scene of such a gruesome occurrence. But after a few moments of hard assery, they softened up. After all, I worked for a multi-billion-dollar corporation that brought many jobs and millions of lira to the local economy. After I finished telling them all that I could remember, they related that all the others had told the same story. They said it was a fluke incident, and no one was at fault.

Mostly, they wanted to see the object that seemed to be the cause of the catastrophe. To my astonishment, I had no recollection of where it was.

There was a white void where my memories should have been, as if they had been sucked clear by a vacuum. They searched my room and vehicle but came up empty. They asked permission to search my office, and I agreed, knowing they would have ransacked it whether I approved of it or not.

It took two days and several IVs of fluids for me to recover enough to return to work. Doctors couldn't explain why every person who was nearby when the flame erupted suffered the same strange maladies: dehydration, intestinal distress, and throbbing neuralgia. Corporate sent an insurance investigator to interview me, an angry bean counter who strutted around and squawked like an angry rooster about the time lost on the project and the hefty settlement they had to pay Ahmet's family.

They had no reason to fire me, as I had always performed well under pressure. I had to hire a new set of workers, as not one of my previous group would return. I also doubled down on my efforts. Even with the tragedy, I got the project finished under budget and only one day late. I tried to make it appear to senior execs that it was my work ethic and expertise that got the project done so expediently.

But it was more Ahmet's death and the loss of the priceless artifact that made me want to get out of there as fast as possible. The part that hurt was the fact that I was never even able to open the box and see what irreplaceable objects were stored inside. To have such a wondrous piece of history in my own two hands, then to have it mysteriously disappear was a mystery that would haunt me forever.

I couldn't wait to get back to Istanbul and see my wife again. Hiraya was as gorgeous as any woman I'd ever known back in the States and many times more exotic. Her name meant "May Your Dreams Come True." For me, those words couldn't ring more genuinely.

I met her in the Philippines when I was building a road that connected her village to the nearest large town. I couldn't sleep one night. A repeating dream kept waking me up, a beautiful vision that fled from my memory as soon as I awakened.

I couldn't bear it any longer. The phantasms left me restless, yearning for something I never knew I needed. I got dressed and left my quarters, driving down a dirt trail in the middle of nowhere. That's where I spotted her, standing motionless amongst the trees, her eyes glowing in my headlights. She was supple and lithe with long black tresses as smooth as silk, so statuesque that I couldn't believe she was real. I think I fell in love before I even tapped the brakes.

I gave her a ride home. She had soft caramel skin, irresistible dimples that curled up when she smiled, and a giggle that raised goosebumps on the nape of my neck. We rambled along with small talk as if we had known each other for our entire lives. It turned out that she was an orphan, found in the ruins of an old Anito shrine that was built before Europeans arrived to "enlighten" them. Her family raised her as one of their own. They didn't have the material goods that Americans take for granted, but they welcomed me with open arms. She could be as distant as a mirage one moment, then blaze into a sensual goddess the next.

Soon I was spending every free moment I had in her tiny village, a collection of huts, many without electricity and running water. The inhabitants were wary of me at first but warmed up after I began bringing carloads of gifts: clothing, tools, food, and other things they were in dire need of. I obeyed all their laws and customs of courtship. I couldn't bear to lose Hiraya, my one and only true love.

I never thought I'd end up being one of those semi-mental clowns who get all mushy about love and weddings, but I went all hardcore, trying to be Son-in-Law of the Year. The ceremony was serene and unforgettable, as our lives together had been since then.

I craved her terribly during these long assignments, but she would visit me often, and when she couldn't, she sent a ton of selfies to remind me of what I was missing. She stood there waiting for me at the airport, dressed in her chicest new outfit. I could always detect her in a crowd. My eyes were instinctively drawn to her form. Ravishing yet still the innocent young girl I had stumbled upon six years earlier. The sight of her reminded me that Hiraya was the only treasure I truly needed.

To hell with my luggage. I left orders to have it delivered later. She drove me as fast as possible back to our humble home. The company paid well; our place was palatial compared to most of the rest of the city. She said I seemed different, a bit paler and more distracted. I supposed I still hadn't recovered completely from the mishap.

We made love immediately, then several times more until the darkness of night fell. We never bothered to turn on the lights, letting the cool of the evening replenish our bodies. I was older than Hiraya, but she seemed to appreciate that. I wasn't some immature punk who was only around for the sex and none of the responsibilities or commitment.

I worked hard to provide for her, and she reciprocated in whatever ways she could. She kept the house and finances in perfect order and made sure my favorite foods were selected for meals. She made my life complete, and I believe she felt the same way about me. Except for children. She had always wanted a family, but I was dead set against it. Why ruin the perfection of our existence with a bunch of meddling kids?

I understood her loneliness and her desire to bring new life into the world, so I kept telling her to wait a few more years. It was always a few more years. Each time I told her that, I could see in her eyes that she believed me less and less. She would turn away with a gentle sigh that could bring a tear to even the most heartless dude.

The next morning, I awoke refreshed and as happy as I had been since Ahmet's demise. I was hoping for a repeat of the previous night's debauchery, but morning sex was not Hiraya's deal. Morning breath grossed her out, and the new day brought her new errands to run. She had her own things that she wanted to accomplish.

She left a note on her pillow telling me to expect her back at around eleven. I had slept late, and it was already half past ten, so her return was imminent. I took a shower and had a quick snack: Halka Tatlisi, a delicious pastry that I always called a Turkish churro, which made me smile but made Hiraya shake her head.

I went to my study to catch up on mail. I always thought calling it a study sounded pretentious, but that's what the maid called it, and that's what Hiraya and our friends and family called it. It was just a room in the back of the house where I kept all of my stuff.

Inside was an expensive antique china cabinet where I kept all of my sports memorabilia, including bobbleheads of the Bears, Blackhawks, and Bulls. On the walls I hung framed posters of Casablanca, Lawrence of Arabia, and other classic films set in the Middle East. It also had a pristine wooden desk where my laptop sat abandoned and collecting dust.

I never knew why I kept the room locked. It wasn't like I had anything of immense value in there or anything I wanted to keep secret from Hiraya. Maybe because it was so American in there. And immature. All the action figures and model cars were a little embarrassing to let people from other countries come in and roll their eyes at.

10

I unlocked the door and strode in with an ear-to-ear grin on my face. It was the one place in my overseas life where I felt at home. I could forget how isolated I was, being so far away from the States for so long. I always acted as if the great distance and the different cultures didn't bother me, but deep down it did. But not in my study. It was my safe space, where I felt as if I were back in Chicago.

Everyone has experienced some type of shock before. Someone sneaking up from behind and scaring them. A car backfiring, sounding like gunfire. Actual gunfire. But all the surprises and stunning moments I had felt in my lifetime combined together paled in comparison to what I felt at that instant.

For there, sitting on my desk, was the relic.

It wasn't wrapped in cardboard with postage stamps on it. Nor was it in an attaché case as if some shady character had smuggled it through customs. It just sat on my desk like it belonged there, like it was supposed to be there. Like my study was its home.

I bit my tongue instead of the churro. My knees buckled, and I nearly collapsed into a heap on the floor. I jumped across the room in a single bound, yet I was afraid to touch it, afraid the tiniest contact would make it disappear again. Was this a hallucination? It had to be. I thought by now it had been sold on the black market to some billionaire as an addition to his collection of antiques and oddities. But no one had any real clue what mysterious hellhole it had vanished into.

I had to touch it. I slid my finger closer, approaching painstakingly, the way I acted when I petted the tiger at the animal sanctuary years before. Only when I finally connected with it, my fingers grazing its surface, did I truly believe it was real. I finally possessed the trophy artifact to match my trophy wife.

My feeling of elation was hard to describe. Pride and ecstasy welled up in my body and engulfed me. This was better than sex, better than winning the lottery. Better than my dead relatives coming back to life.

As I ran my finger along the engraved course of the comet toward the mountains, an electrical impulse swelled though my body, something I hadn't felt back at the jobsite.

It was as if the chest had chosen me as its owner. I could feel the warmth and camaraderie it had for me. An unearthly bond had formed between us, unbreakable and everlasting. We belonged to each other. We were consorts, more than man and wife. I would never leave its side. We would be together forever.

"Kenneth?" my wife said from the doorway. Jolted, my fingers snapped away from the chest, and the malignant connection disappeared as if a hypnotist had snapped his fingers and awoken me from a deep trance. A feeling of embarrassment worse than anything I could have imagined flushed over my face. Worse than someone catching me knocking one off.

"Hiraya?" I replied, and she wandered over.

"Didn't you hear me?"

"Yes, of course."

"I repeated your name three or four times before you answered me."

"I . . . I, what?"

She touched my arm, and I trembled as if from shock, then slumped away.

"Are you OK, sweetheart. Are you still feeling some ill effects from the accident?"

"Accident? No, no accident," I mumbled.

"Sit down, honey. Get off your feet and relax. Maybe we overstrained ourselves last night."

I barely heard her and couldn't fathom how to reply. I pointed to the relic to change the subject. "How did this get in here?"

"What is it?" she asked. "Where did it come from?"

"You don't know? You didn't leave it in here?"

"Of course not, darling. I can't even remember where the spare key to this room is."

"Well, then how did it get in here? Did the maid—"

"No, Fatima would never come in here. We both know this is your little hideaway. Neither of us would dare disturb your little dolls and race cars," she laughed, a bit more derisively than I would have liked.

I grabbed her arm, a little harder than I meant to. "Don't you know what this is? This is the artifact I told you about. The box we found under the slab at Urfa."

Hiraya's expression changed dramatically. She looked angry and hurt that I had seized her so forcefully, but she was mostly stunned by the presence of the vanished treasure.

"That's impossible. You told me it was lost forever. How did it suddenly appear in your study, thirteen hundred kilometers away?"

"I know. I know. But look at it. Isn't it exquisite? Look at the carving."

"What's inside?" she asked, her eyes glowing like the first moment I saw her.

"I don't know. Not a person alive does. But we're going to find out right now."

I opened my drawer and pulled out a box cutter I used to open packages. My hands quivering, I cut the four pieces of leather that tied the lid down. Then I lifted the top section off the slightly indented lower half.

I might have been mistaken, but I thought I saw a slight mist seep out from the crevices as the box was opened for the first time in millennia. There was definitely an odor, a mixture of denatured alcohol, asphalt, and rotten peanut butter. I was so tense; I nearly crushed the fragile wood with my fingers.

A tingling feeling at the top of my head sent shivers coursing through my arms. What could be inside? Scrolls relating the history of a people so ancient that the world had forgotten them? A king's ransom in precious stones? The secret of life itself? Or was it empty? The first practical joke in history, played by Neolithic jesters, intended to humiliate and disappoint someone so far in the future that genealogy scarcely had a connection between them.

But there was something inside. My mind lurched as the contents came into view. Small circular coins, each close to an inch in diameter, made from a weird alloy that I had never seen before. But how did those archaic hominids forge metal when they didn't even have a pot to piss in?

Then I remembered that the ancients would work with meteoric metals found after they crashed to earth. Those were the only alloys known to humankind at the time. They could have heated and shaped the disks over a fire.

But why would they need currency?

They were arranged perfectly in little circular slots carved into the wood, like those blue cardboard coin collector folders that nerds owned as kids to hold their old nickels and dimes.

Yet what was truly intriguing were the markings, vivid embossments far too advanced for primitive humanoids to have created. The symbols upon the coins were like nothing I had ever seen. They were created ages before cuneiform but were much more complex, similar to ancient Chinese yet somehow felt more meaningful.

"Oh, my, Kenneth. They're spectacular," Hiraya said.

I nodded in agreement, even though her words barely registered in my head. The carvings on the coins seemed to radiate. There was a history in each one, an epic story begging to be told. Each design was its own character.

Hiraya couldn't resist. She extended her willowy index finger and touched one of them.

"No!" I yelled with a touch of anger, but it was too late. I tried to tell myself I was mad because the coins might have been fragile, and she could have damaged them. But I knew it was because I wanted to be the first to feel them.

Her hand jerked away immediately. She looked stunned—and a little scared.

"Wait, what's that?" she asked. I looked, and there was an undeniable glow to the coin she had just touched. It wasn't from the angle of the light or a trick of the senses. The symbol almost . . . came to life.

"How did it feel?" I asked.

"Warm yet cold."

"How could it be both?"

"The coin was cold, but I felt a definite warmth from the lines of the symbol itself."

"Really? You're not just making that up?"

"No, not on my soul. I could feel the imprint of its marking almost vibrating."

That was all I needed to hear. I brought my finger to bear on a coin next to the one she had fondled. It hit me immediately, a strange force, similar to the way one electromagnet ensnares another. It sucked me to it, and I could sense every curve of the symbol's heat.

Whatever the essence inside our bodies is—the soul, the intelligence, the energy of life—whatever I had inhabiting my flesh and bones reveled in the connection. Just the thought of a new form of existence, a new state of material essence, invigorated a dreamy bliss from deep inside my inner being, the likes of which I had never felt before, something that perhaps no human had felt in twelve thousand years.

"Oh, my lord. It's like nothing the modern world has ever witnessed," I exclaimed.

Hiraya wrapped her arm around my shoulders, and I could feel the sexual vitality emanating from within her. I knew she felt it as well, for I saw a hint of embarrassment flash across her face, the kind that strikes when lust hits us unexpectedly. She must have seen the same thing in my face for a fleeting moment. Once lovers see the same passion in their partner's face, any discomfort quickly passes.

But I also saw her excitement, her thrill of discovering something new and potentially earth-shattering. We couldn't help ourselves. We touched each of the coins many times. With each caress, more of the vitality sparkled through our veins.

We were enjoying all the mind-altering effects of tripping without the speediness and paranoid delusions. Our brains and bodies experienced a cosmic awakening, as if these coins were the gateway to a new form of existence, a vitality no modern human had experienced.

We decided to remove all of them and place them on the desk. We each seemed to have our favorites. Was it the shapes of the symbols or the sensations we felt when we palmed them into our hands? Or a combination of both? We swirled them around on the smooth mahogany surface like children playing with new toys.

It was then that Hiraya came to an incredible conclusion.

"They fit together!" she cried.

"What do you mean?" I asked.

"The symbols. The shapes on the coins. Look."

Hiraya twirled two coins toward each other until they touched. It took me a few seconds, but then I saw exactly what she meant.

"Good god!" I shouted.

"They're like pieces of a jigsaw puzzle. See how the end of this one fits perfectly into the crevice of the other?"

She was so right. We spun around coin after coin, and they all seemed to have their own magical playmates, practically begging to be enjoined.

"We have to solve the puzzle," she said.

"But how?"

She held up her cell phone and smiled. I knew what she meant. I grabbed one of the coins and used the phone to take a picture of it. She photographed some of the others. Soon we had a complete collection of the entire set.

We transferred the photos to my laptop and then went to work. None of the symbols matched anything on the Internet. Google be damned, we had hit the jackpot. I used imaging software to remove the coin shapes and enhance the symbols.

Once that was done, Hiraya and I toyed with the different pieces, rearranging them on the computer screen until they fit another. Then I added a layer, and we continued. A shape was forming as the puzzle grew larger and larger. It was lackluster, just an amorphous blob with no intrigue to it, no exalted pattern that made us exclaim with shock.

After a long while, Hiraya yawned. Not a real yawn, where I could tell she was tired. It was a phony one, the kind that signaled she wanted me to come to bed.

I was so excited, I had lost track of time. It had been seven hours since we opened the box. I could see why she wanted to pass out, but I was way too revved up for naptime. She swiveled her dexterous fingers up along the sides and the nape of my neck, sighing with that sensual softness that made me want to follow her anywhere.

But this was the find of the millennia. How could she expect me to go to bed now?

"Aren't you tired of these silly pennies when you know you could be upstairs playing with me?" she asked, rubbing up against me until I couldn't help but pay attention.

"In a few minutes, sweetheart. I'll be right up. I promise."

She sauntered across the room as delicately as a doe in the field. She pursed her lips and flashed a naked thigh at me. The look in her eyes made me melt.

"Kenneth . . ."

"Just a few more minutes," I said. "I swear to God."

I was telling the truth. Sort of. I couldn't leave those precious artifacts until the puzzle was complete. Then I would race upstairs as quickly as my feet could take me. Hiraya smiled at me and then slinked out of the room. She hid behind the wall and then took off her flimsy sundress and tossed it back through the doorway.

For the life of me, I couldn't understand how she could walk away from such a discovery, especially with how the coins caused such enthralling emotions in both of us. But I also felt the rush of blood caused by those same emotions. I would need a release of some kind very soon.

Without Hiraya, the enchanting puzzle began to feel more like a tragic chore. All the pieces fit together one by one, but all they were building was a boring pattern of brown goo. It was as if all the energy was being drained from my adventure and from the coins.

I was heartbeats away from joining my wife in the bedroom. Just a few more sections, and the image would be finished. She couldn't blame me for staying down there for that.

It was then that I noticed my laptop was beginning to get warm. As another piece fit, even the keys started to get hot. After another, the screen seemed to electrify. The pixels rippled and sparked. I felt like a necromancer adding the final ingredients to a potion in a cauldron.

I was down to the final symbol. The computer was going crazy, sliding around on the desk until I had to steady it with one hand while manipulating it with the other. Smoke poured from the fan area, and the touchpad began to melt.

But for whatever reason, I wasn't afraid. Or maybe I was just too embroiled in this hornet's nest of a conundrum to care. The image was still a blob of nothingness when I guided the last symbol into its rightful place in the center. Right where the heart should be in my imagination.

That's when all hell broke loose.

The fathomless image swallowed its final section and erupted in an implosion of ecstasy. The shape transmuted, pulsating with inner life, almost breathing through the computer's vents. The screen bulged out as the shape began procreating itself inside the machine.

Microchips and software combined to spawn the most horrifying creature the universe had ever seen. The unbearably filthy smell of a million-year-old cesspool poured out from the fan, making me heave chunks everywhere. The sounds of billions of tortured souls suffering in hell emitted from the speakers, sizzling my brain through my ears.

Then the sight of the monster, the bringer of all evil, the creator of all torment, the beginning and end of all suffering in the universe, assailed my eyes. It was as if someone was holding sharp pokers over a flame till the metal almost melted, then jammed them into my orbs. The very sight of it caused me to twist my head away. I even heard a crackling sound and felt a twinge, as if I had injured a vertebra.

The sheer agony of the creature's presence ripped the soul from my body and sent it screaming into another dimension. I sensed it being torn asunder, its spiritual molecules vaporized in the most excruciating way imaginable.

Then it attacked me, pouring out of the computer screen like a tidal wave of putrescence. It bowled me over. My chair tipped over, and my back slammed into the floor. The creature strangled and suffocated me, swarming over my face so that none of my five senses worked except touch. I clawed at it with my fingers until my nails tore right off, but the beast would not be denied.

It finally inhabited me, taking over the vacant hole left by my lost spirit. Every one of the most horrible experiences anyone had ever imagined recurred over and over inside my helpless frame. All the excretions and poisons and toxic wastes of a trillion planets colonized inside my worthless carcass.

I was now the thing that the old ones had buried, hoping no one would ever discover. Diabolus, the Unspeakable One. The cause of all evil in humanity. The beast who chased the first humans from the Garden of Eden. It had rained down from the heavens thousands of years ago and wreaked havoc on any primitive with whom it came into contact.

Whatever mumbo jumbo spell our ancestors conceived to trap it under that rock was lost to history. It took humankind's newest folly, the personal computer, to bring it back to life. And now I could sense its purpose. I could feel the one thing it truly desired.

"Diabolus!" Hiraya called from the upstairs bedroom. "Come to me, my lord."

Hiraya. She had been found as an orphan wandering around an ancient temple. She was the one who had told me about this job in Urfa. She was the one who figured out the pieces fit together like a puzzle.

She had always wanted children, but I had refused her.

It looked as if she had found a surrogate father to supply her with the offspring she desired. I was simply the vessel.

As I rushed up the stairs to be with her, I begged God to have mercy on my soul. But no deity in heaven or hell would forgive me for what I was about to do.

Elliptical Journey

*T*he local health club could be a little spooky at 2:30 a.m. I would zoom up the street because there was nobody on the road, squeak into the best spot in the parking lot right next to the front door because it was completely empty, walk up and see a brightly lit gym filled with the latest and most expensive weightlifting and exercise equipment, and yet the whole place was as desolate as a graveyard. I had to use a phone app to buzz myself in, then strolled through the double doors that magically opened before me. Loud pop music assaulted my eardrums, blaring for no one to hear. It was unnerving that there wasn't even a person at the desk to check me in.

Once inside, I had the run of the place. I could invite all my friends to bring beer and throw a wild party. Who was gonna stop me? Although I guess they must have had video cameras running at all times to make sure such things didn't happen. So, I was in the middle of that vacant place, as deserted as a graveyard, but I realized someone was always watching me. It was a paranoid delusional nightmare.

All that didn't bother me much, though. I was a manager at a popular nearby restaurant. We stayed open till 2:00 a.m., but it was really quiet for the last hour or so. I usually let the staff go home early when it was like that, so it was just me by myself. I enjoyed it. No more messed up orders or incessant whining from apathetic employees. And I had room to breathe after a long, hectic day filled with Karens and Kyles and their uncontrollable, Ritalin-charged offspring. I would wind down and get things set for the following day's shift.

But a lot of my time was spent at my desk on my computer dealing with shipping and receiving, payroll, and corporate BS. So, most nights when I had the energy, I locked up, dropped the cash off at the bank, and hit the gym. Blew off the day's aggravation and tightened my abs. The pies where I worked were irresistible, so I needed to work off as many calories as possible. I was single, so having a rocking bod when I went to the beach or a barbeque helped when I tried to hook up with someone.

I'd been on a slow burn with that lately. I was twenty-seven and pretty decent looking. If I wasn't so self-deprecating, I would say I was handsome. And I was steadily employed, which helped. But it wasn't exactly a job that was gonna impress any really fine women. Even though I spent my days barking out orders and dealing with customers, deep down, I'm an introvert. And hitting on women is like a standup comedian doing his act on stage. Mess up just one punchline, and you lose your audience's attention.

The worst part of my job was having to ax workers for not showing up or for stealing from the cash register. Some of them almost deserved a real ax! In a small town, that could give a person a bad rep. I'd be trying to hit on an attractive young lady, then they would find out who I was. Suddenly, they'd be like, "You fired my best friend's sister!", and they would storm off.

Still, I always reminded myself that I was alive, healthy, and not in prison, so I was doing a lot better than some of the people I went to high school with. Normal life is bad enough. I had one friend who got too drunk at a party at the ocean and drowned. Another was flattened into roadkill by a speeding Peterbilt. And if you add in drugs, bullets, and juvie hall, the overall health of my graduating class plummeted. I tried to stay as far away from such trouble as I could. But with only 200 kids in the whole district, it was impossible to avoid it completely. You had to deal with the good and the bad and a few who were too good to be true.

Like Kaylee. She was so hot she was untouchable. And she was so sweet and kind that jealous girls claimed she was a big faker. But she wasn't. I could tell by her angelic smile that she was a good person. She moved here from Texas right before senior year. But somehow, we didn't have one class together, so I never got a chance to get to know her. When I saw her at parties, she always stayed in a group and never strayed off where a predatory dude might try to cut her off from the pack and coerce her into doing something she didn't want to do. As the new girl in town, she never knew who she could trust.

She could have trusted me. I'm one of those weird guys who actually likes to treat girls like ladies. It almost seems as if I'm part of a dying breed, unlike the grabby macho clowns who seem to get all the action. I'm not a fumble-fingered stutter-fuck either. I couldn't understand why I didn't click more often with the opposite sex. I guess scientists know what they're talking about. Girls can sense desperation. They're attracted to guys who already have other women in their lives. Think about it. They must be doing something right.

I used to be that guy, but after my last relationship, which at eighteen months was the longest I ever had, something broke down. She dumped me, and I was miserable. Females pick up on those little things, and the more it drags out, the harder it is to regain your confidence. I lost my skills, broke off eye contact, fidgeted way too much. And worst of all, I started slumping like a nerd at a Star Wars convention.

That's when I really started concentrating at the gym. More deadlifts, squats, and reverse flies to strengthen my posture. More aerobic training to stop my nervous squirming. I also practiced talking to women about their workouts at the gym. Not in a sexual way, just as friends interested in getting fitter. And it was starting to work. I felt myself making gains in the dating department. Things were looking up.

But not with Kaylee. For whatever reason, I couldn't bring myself to rap with her. Maybe it was because we never connected at school, and I felt trapped in the friend zone. Maybe it was because in the back of my mind I felt unworthy. When you put a woman too high on a pedestal, sometimes she starts looking down on you like a peasant.

That was why I was so excited when she started working out at the same gym at the same time I did. I guess she got off work as a bartender at a local watering hole at two in the morning and drove straight here. It was a dream come true. I would usually get there right before her and start on the ellipticals. She came a few minutes later and ran on the treadmills, which were right in front of the windows. Lithe as a doe, racing right in front of my eyes. She was a goddess in a ponytail, wearing a bodysuit that highlighted every exquisite muscle.

I was so shocked when I saw her stroll in the first time, my tongue went numb, and my brain went haywire. She wandered right past me, glancing ever so slightly my way. It was just enough to get a tight convo started. We had never been alone together or so close before, so I couldn't come up with anything more than a "Wussup?" I could see the tiny bit of interest in her eyes ride off into the sunset. She hopped onto her favorite machine and raced away. Even worse, I couldn't help but ogle her. I could tell she spotted my sad puppy dog expression staring at her reflection in the glass. If I wasn't in the "zone" before, I was buried neck deep in it now.

So, ever since then, we just said "Hey" to each other. She still smiled at me every night we met. She even winked once in a while. So, in my mind, there was still a chance. I just figured I had to devise a brilliant, infallible scheme to make her fall madly in love with me, using only my quick wit and sexy demeanor. Fat chance. Most of the time I spent the next half hour trying not to stare at her gorgeous physique. Lately, I'd even been quitting my routine early to avoid the embarrassment. I'd go straight into free weights at the back of the gym instead, my mind struggling to find a way out of this platonic hell.

But that was then, and this is now, and it's unlikely we'll ever see each other again because about a week ago, the day before her twenty-seventh birthday, Kaylee disappeared off the face of the earth. Her coworkers found her car still parked at the bar where she tended at closing time. The door was wide open, the keys on the ground next to her purse, and her purse's contents spilled across the asphalt, including her wallet with cash and credit cards. The only video cameras that functioned were over the cash registers to protect the owners from employee theft. There was nothing to protect employees from sicko criminals in the parking lot.

Sheriff Bradlee put on a good show for the media. He was always a fair guy, unlike some of the other officers who enjoyed screwing with the poor kids from the area. Seems like some guys become cops just so they can bully other people around. But Bradlee treated everyone fairly, from the rich folks down to the trailer trash. Maybe that's why he had been elected four times straight. He spoke in front of the reporter's cameras as if he was the news anchor for Channel 5. Stoic but with a hint of enthusiasm. Pragmatic but with a glimmer of hope in his voice. Something in his eyes made a person feel as if he would get the job done, that we could trust him to find Kaylee or at least her killer.

Gossip flew around town like empty plastic shopping bags in the wind. The most reliable busybodies were saying that the authorities had no real clues. Joe at the barber shop and Mary the post office lady believed it was a random kidnapping by some whack job. Truck driver probably or some criminal lowlife traveling through. The police interviewed all the usual suspects and got nothing but a mess of finger pointing, trails that led them everywhere but ended up nowhere.

They had no choice but to begin investigating us upstanding citizens. Some people feigned outrage, and others, like me, understood it was part of their job. I wish I could have been more helpful to them, but I had picked that night of all nights to go on a massive tequila binge. It strikes me once every few months when I know I have a couple of days off work. One deep, heavy slug out of a bottle of Patron, and I forget everything. Complete blackout after that. Just one long vacation from reality. Couldn't tell you if I went fishing or hit a casino.

I woke up in bed naked, not even wearing a pair of boxers, which was totally out of character. I figured I had gotten lucky with some girl at a bar, and she had taken off before I arose. I checked around the house and was elated to find my Holy Trinity on the counter: wallet, phone, and keys. Nothing else was missing except my favorite running shoes and a pair of jeans. I figured I had left them in the girl's car because I would have been in no condition to drive. So, I had lucked out. She could have emptied my bank account.

The cops did their due diligence and ended up with the proverbial load of squat. They said it was unlikely they'd ever find her. I didn't want to get involved, so I simply told the patrolman who interviewed me that I spent the night at home flipping channels. Guys have such short attention spans nowadays; I didn't even have to mention what program I had been watching. He didn't seem that interested. It was as if because she wasn't born a local, whatever happened to her wasn't a major concern. It pissed me off, but what could I do? You mess with cops down here and they spend the next five years harassing you until you learn your lesson. They live for that shit.

What a tragic end for such a wonderful girl. So, from then on, my workouts were a little lonely. And sad. I couldn't separate the messed-up feelings I had inside about the whole situation, the morbid realization that she had likely been raped and murdered and my depression about her being lost to me forever. The combination of the two made me sick to my stomach. Why are our emotions so fucked up? I felt horrible for her, but my own emotions got all tangled together with that. I felt heartless and narcissistic.

Going to the gym every day after that was a real bummer. I didn't even feel like exercising. Some monster had snatched her life out from under her. Probably tortured her. They'll rarely speak to a guy about it, but I'm certain that's probably every woman's worst fear. How do they even exist day to day, knowing every time they walk outside, some pervert could end their time on earth over a moment's pleasure. Such men are the true monsters of the world.

And why was I even working out anymore? Kaylee was my dream girl. The rest of the ladies in town paled before her. I was ready to give it all up. Drop my gym membership. Go out partying all the time. Grow a beard and a beer gut and settle into a life of cheap liquor and even cheaper women. There wasn't any point anymore without her. Morose and frustrated, I was about to jump off the machine and leave for the last time.

But then I noticed something strange. What the hell was that? A wisp of fog. An inaudible whisper in my ear as it passed by. An ethereal essence taking form before my incredulous eyes. Suddenly, from out of nowhere, Kaylee's ghost took shape, right on the very spot where she had always run. On her favorite machine. Jogging at a steady pace, as if she had never gone away.

My mouth opened slow and wide, like an automatic garage door, and not because I was short of breath. My left foot slipped off the pedal of my elliptical, and I fell right off the machine. I stumbled till my knees hit the ground, banging my shoulder against the machine next to me. Scared that I would lose her, I bounced right back up. But she was still there, racing like a thoroughbred, as if she had never disappeared. But she had. How was this possible?

The fear I should have felt was overwhelmed by a sense of relief. I had felt so much guilt about her homicide but seeing her like that made it vanish in an instant. Kaylee was here again, with me. Even though I could see right through her, she had a tangible spirit. At first, she was almost black and white, translucent, like a ghost from an old horror movie. But I gathered my nerve and stepped closer, and she became more and more alive. Color returned to her spectral image, even though I could see the other machines right through her.

Finally, I couldn't stand it any longer. I approached so stealthily, I could have reached out and petted a wild deer. Then I did touch her, the tip of my shaking finger crossing into the celestial plane. I hoped she would come back to life somehow. Instead, she turned to me with a face of sheer terror, as if Michelangelo had sculpted the expression of the most beautiful woman in history the split second before she was brutally slaughtered. Then her wild eyes sizzled at me like two laser beams, glowering with all the fear, anger, and hatred any human could muster. Her scream was so shrill that my ears started ringing.

She jumped back off her machine and crouched in the corner, panting like a scared kid. Her face transformed into a painful mess. She had been beaten so brutally; I could hardly bear to look at her. Fat lips, blackened eyes, swollen cheeks. But it was Kaylee, looking so frightened, so bewildered.

"What the fuck?" she said in a wraithlike voice from another realm that echoed inside my skull. From the Great Beyond, I guess, that eerie domain where phantoms and poltergeists are trapped, caught forever in an endless cycle.

"Kaylee, it's me. Jim from the gym," I said, realizing how dumb that sounded. Her terror softened from totally freaked out to a kind of morose disbelief.

"You can see me?"

"Yes. I'm so sorry. Can you tell me who killed you?"

"Killed me? Am I dead?"

"I . . . I think you are. You're practically invisible."

These sad circumstances didn't seem to be registering in her brain. She was having a difficult time understanding what was happening. Then Kaylee stared at her gossamer arm and realized she was truly dead. A citizen of the afterlife. And nothing could ever bring her back to life.

"Why am I at the gym? What am I doing here?"

"I don't know. You just suddenly appeared out of nowhere."

She looked so lost, the way you would imagine someone in between worlds would appear, trying to piece together where her soul was supposed to be.

"What happened to me?"

"You were kidnapped from the bar parking lot a week ago. No one has found a trace of you since then."

"A week? I remember something. I remember . . . Oh my God!"

Her face crinkled into a mess of pain, as if memories of her fate came flooding back to her, and none of them were pleasant. She grabbed at her face and her guts and her crotch, wailing so mournfully I wanted to cry. Then she curled into a ball on the floor, rolling back and forth, attempting to exorcise all these brutal memories from her consciousness.

I tried to comfort her, stroking her hair. Touching this celestial being felt magical, like the vapor billowing from the exit vent of a dryer on laundry day, only more intense. It was like frigid liquid gas, almost magnetic. Goosebumps rose across my entire body with such force that they actually hurt. Thousands of pinching hair follicles, all reaching toward her. It took the longest time, but her agony finally subsided. She stopped rocking, just murmured wistfully and stared into the distance.

"Can you tell me who did this to you?" I asked.

"No. He was wearing a mask."

"Can you tell me where he buried you?"

"Buried me? How did you know that?" she cried, sliding away from me till her back flattened against the wall. She stared at me as if I was her attacker. If I wasn't so shocked, I would have been trying to figure out why her ghostly form stopped at the firmness of the sheetrock.

"I just guessed, I guess. Weren't you buried somewhere?"

She stared out the window like an amnesia victim trying to piece her life back together, only all her pieces were scattered across a transcendent abyss. Her ethereal brain had to stretch beyond her faculties and gather it all back, follow the bits of lost memories like a trail of breadcrumbs. Where her reflection should have been was a silhouette of blackness, an ebony shadow blocking out anything that should have been visible outside.

"Woods. Cabin."

"Well, that's good. We have a place to start. Did you recognize it? Had you ever been there before?"

"Old. Broken windows. Holes in the floor. Splinters."

"Can you move? Can you take me back there?"

"I don't want to go. He'll hurt me again."

"I don't think he can hurt you anymore. But you can hurt him. You can get revenge."

I tried to take her by the hand to help her up, but she pulled away as if I were a criminal. She raised herself up, higher than rationally possible, floating inches above the carpet.

"Lead me there. He'll never hurt you again. Take me to where he left you."

She still looked deathly afraid of me but glided straight through the plate glass. I had to run around to the doors and catch up to her. I got in my car and pounded the gas because Kaylee was already almost out of sight down the desolate road. I sped after her, but she was nowhere to be found. I drove up and down side-streets, sped along frontage roads, even drove over embankments onto lawns near forested areas, but she was gone.

Then, out of nowhere, her spirit reappeared in the passenger seat of my car. I screamed, swerved, and hit a small tree.

"Son of a bitch!"

There she sat, glowing right next to me, a chilly mist that had no sensation of humidity shrouding her body. Her presence shot tingles up and down my right side, yet her form left no indentation in the cushions. My mind swirled, unable to comprehend this insane horror movie playing out in my vehicle. I had to check my drawers to make sure I hadn't wet them.

"That way. I think it's that way," she said, pointing south toward a swampy section of the county. I backed up and wheeled around, leaving slivers of my front bumper on the turf behind us. I kept driving anywhere she directed. There were a bunch of abandoned shacks out there, some fairly new, others old and dormant for decades. Flooding over recent years had rendered the roads there nearly impossible to navigate on a daily basis. Luckily, I had purchased a bayou-friendly four-by-four with all-wheel drive a few years back and tricked it out, so it could travel into most marshy parishes and have no problems getting home.

"Why did you show up at the gym? Weren't you supposed to go into the light or something?" I asked, vainly hoping it was because she wanted to see me one last time.

"It's what I did in life, wasn't it? I guess I was haunting it. I just felt it was time to go to the gym."

Why would a ghost be following a schedule? She appeared right around the time she always would on the way home from the bar. Was she actually repeating the things she did in life? The thought of having to go back to work at the restaurant every day after I died caused a nasty shiver that made me shift in my seat. As if having the apparition of my dreams scintillating in the chair next to me wasn't freaking me out enough.

Seeing her the way she was evoked pangs of anxious guilt inside me, starting in my shoulders and settling down around my heart. Why did she have to die? Because of a rapist. A perverted animal who ravaged and murdered girls to satisfy his sick urges. Why didn't such people ever admit such depraved impulses when they were younger? Because they wanted those feelings. Needed those experiences. They loved having such brutal desires inside, and they couldn't wait for their next chance to do it again. I know I've had urges to have rough sex. Testosterone combined with the frustrations and anger of everyday life can create a powder keg of uncontrollable lust.

Yet I could never understand how those monsters could live with themselves. I felt remorse for what happened to her, and I had nothing to do with it. Maybe because I was also jealous of whoever got away with it. He got to have sex with the only girl I ever loved. Where did such demented cravings come from? Having her alone in the car with me sent my libido into some bizarre sixth gear I had never experienced before. My breathing became heavy, my palm sweat making the steering wheel slippery. The blood coursed everywhere, to my brain, my limbs, my chest. I could smell her, that scent that always drove me crazy as she strolled past me to talk to someone else, some asshole guy who didn't deserve her. But now I finally had her all to myself. I slowed down and turned to her, eager to—

"There it is!" she wailed. I was happy to have found it but also miserable because that was the spot where it all happened, where her young life had been snuffed out like a birthday candle. Her killer never sang her a song. Never gave her a present. She would never grow another year older. Never have children or get married or sit chatting with her gray-haired, wrinkly old girlfriends. She had simply been dumped there by some ruthless pig. I hit the brakes and looked forward. What I saw shocked me.

"Oh my god. It's Sonny's place," I said.

I knew that cottage. A distant cousin of mine lived there until hurricane floods made it impossible to occupy year-round. It was still in good shape, a shotgun shack with dark green wooden siding and a ridged roof. A door in the front led straight to the door in the back. Kitchen, bathroom, and two bedrooms. The gabled front porch acted as the sitting room. I had spent a lot of time there as a kid, so it was unimaginable that this was where everything went down.

"Who's Sonny? Why do you know this house?"

"My cousin used to live here. But I haven't been here for—"

"For what?"

I wanted to say years, but then I stopped myself. I knew that was a lie. I loved to go four-wheeling in those woods when I drank tequila. Skid around in the slop, blast some tuneage, scream out the windows to let off steam. The night Kaylee went missing, I was out there. I had even gone looking for that place. I had a lot of fun there when I was a kid. I was trying to bring back old memories of the days before life's problems turned me from a hopeful romantic into a cynical bachelor. But when I was so liquored up and there were no streetlights, it was hard to find the old roads in the middle of the night. I wasn't sure if I had ended up there or not.

"For a while," I lied, exiting the vehicle as fast as possible to avoid answering more questions. What else could I do? She was a ghost, for

Christ sakes. Who knew what she was capable of? She might have been one of those harmless spirits, like Resurrection Mary, just trying to return to the spot she was buried. But with my luck, she was one of those poltergeists who wanted to murder me, so she wouldn't be all alone. Actually, that wouldn't have been so bad. I had loved her from afar for all those years. I didn't just love her body either; I also loved what was inside her. Her essence. The magic that made her Kaylee. We could spend eternity together.

But she had already lost interest in me, drifting around in a daze as if I wasn't even there. Strike another one up for unrequited love. But I understood. She wanted to find herself. I followed her around, figuring she knew where she was going and that she knew exactly where the spot was. I could dig her body up and phone the police. Then a bright tunnel would open up in the sky, and she would fly through it to the afterlife, thanking me for saving her. She would think of me as her hero, the guy who rescued her and sent her off to heaven. I could live with that. That scenario would feed my libido, make me her champion, fuel my fantasies for years to come.

But she was lost and had no clue where to find herself. I started to get edgy. It was hot out there, but the perspiration I was feeling was not hero sweat. It was from worry. Something in the back of my mind was giving me the creeps, turning my stomach. Fragments of my blackout began to reveal themselves like flashes of lightning in my brain. I saw her there. She was screaming and terrified. And I knew where she was buried. My feet reluctantly walked me away from Kaylee toward a section on the other side of the house.

"Over here!" I shouted without thinking. She flew over, anxious to see what I had found. The ground there had been recently dug up. A round, wide mound was already starting to settle back into the earth, but she was under there; I knew it. I went to my truck and grabbed a shovel, which was already crusted with soil. You never know out here when you'll need to dig yourself out of trouble. I dug furiously. Rocks and mud flew everywhere. I couldn't stop myself. I was relentless, as if something inside me needed to find her, to expose her body.

It didn't take long. After a few feet, I struck her foot. It was so wild because Kaylee felt it and winced. She reached down and clutched her floating limb. I got down on my hands and knees and brushed the filth away from her body. She moaned as I caressed it from her flesh. She was ecstatic. We had discovered her corpse. She swirled up and around like a goldfish in a bowl, so happy to have been discovered, freed from the anguish of not knowing what happened to her.

But then I uncovered her face, and when she saw how badly she had been beaten, she began to wail, an unbearable sobbing cry that resounded throughout the woods. A haunting shriek that kept looping back to assail my eardrums over and over in a vicious circle. It was too painful, and I dropped to the turf, rolling on the ground, clutching the sides of my head. It felt as if I was moments from insanity. A few seconds more, and I think I would have snapped. I screamed at her to stop, to tell her she was killing me, but they were mere whispers compared to her caterwauling.

Then she stopped. Not only the screeching, but her ghostly form ceased moving as well, hovering like a statue above her makeshift grave. Her face exhibited a torrent of emotions, from agonizing pain to deranged bewilderment to shock to horrible revelation, then exploding into uncontrollable anger. What was she going through? This didn't seem like the way a ghost would move on to the next life. This was demonic fury, the face of unadulterated vengeance.

"You! You knew exactly where I was buried. You always wanted me but didn't have the guts to go after me. You raped me. Then you murdered me. I'll make what's left of your life a living hell."

She grabbed my throat and squeezed, lifting me four feet off the ground. Her fingernails dug into my neck, red droplets squirting everywhere. Not only did she cut off my airway, it also seemed as if she was draining away whatever oxygen I had inside me. I felt my eyes bulging out of their sockets. My brain was flooded, a torrent of pressure that felt as if my skull was going to burst.

I attempted to rip her hands away, but my entire body from my neck down went limp due to lack of circulation. And why should I try to stop her? I deserved this. I remembered being here. I must have been guilty. How could I be such a monster? How could I traumatize and slaughter the love of my life? I needed to go to hell. I wanted to go there. To suffer the tortures of Satan for committing such a horrible crime. I gave up, wanting her to put me out of my misery.

Suddenly, I heard a coughing sound, then another and another. Her hands loosened their vise-like grip, and we both looked down and saw the impossible. Kaylee's body was moving. She was alive, squirming to free herself from her death pit, desperately sucking in oxygen while choking on dirt. Her ghost lowered us down, and we stood side by side in awe at the incredible sight.

Then a bright light flashed in the distance. Why would the tunnel to heaven appear now? Kaylee was alive.

But it wasn't what I had thought. Two headlights switched on, engines revved, and strobing red-and-blue lights flashed. A police siren screamed in the night. My shadow was spotlighted against the house. Kaylee's ghostly image almost vanished in the brilliance. What the hell was going on?

"Run!" Kaylee cried as her spirit sank down and melded back into her body.

I heard the sounds of impending doom. Even though I was practically blinded, I sensed a huge vehicle speeding toward me. I took off without thinking. Instead of trying to get to my ride, I just made tracks away from the other car. But it quickly caught up to me. I felt it bearing down, and I knew it was about to run me over. So, I took a leap of faith to the right. It swerved toward me but flashed past.

I got back to my feet and made a beeline for my truck. I was only a few feet away, but I could tell the police car was closing in on me, so I dove out of the way again. It smashed into the driver's side of my wheel well, crushing the axle and putting it out of commission. I sprinted back across the marshy ground, hoping to reach the house as my unknown assailant barreled down upon me.

I reached the front door just as the car struck the railing and flew up the stairs. I tripped and fell as the belly of the beast flew above me. The rickety deck collapsed, and I was pinned under the vehicle's front end. I screamed as the hot undercarriage sizzled on my back. It was lodged at a high angle from the steps. I scratched and scraped at the planks, dragging myself out from under it, then pulled the door open.

As I crawled inside, I realized the vehicle's weight had injured me worse than I thought. My lower body was numb, and I could hardly work my legs. The kitchen where I had played with Hot Wheels and GI Joes now had whips and sex toys hanging from the walls. I squirmed as far as I could, but the vehicle kept coming. It smashed in the door frame, retreated, then careened back and forth again and again until it drove completely into the house itself.

As I dragged myself down the hallway, it crushed the load-bearing partitions of the bedrooms. The beds that I used to sleep in now had handcuffs attached to thick metal rings anchored to the walls. Swords and guns were mounted as trophies.

Huge splinters flew everywhere as the car advanced. Chunks of sheetrock smashed onto my arms and back, the car's wheels now making indented pathways through the flooring. If not for the hallway walls holding it back, the car would have pulverized me.

I kept crawling, and it kept crushing. I could hear the driver's deranged laughter as he tormented me. He seemed to be enjoying turning the beautiful old cottage into kindling as much as he relished torturing me. Light fixtures fell from the ceiling. Heavy old picture frames plunged like the blades of guillotines from above, cutting into the floor around me. Dust and exhaust fumes choked me till I thought I would pass out.

I made it to the back door and tried to grab the knob to escape. I turned it, but my sweaty hands made it nearly impossible. I heard the cop car's gears grinding as he made one last attempt to kill me. It rammed me in the back, slamming me into the door. The door flung open, but then the flooring collapsed. I fell several feet to the ground below, as did the car. It drove after me, but the wheels were too high, and the undercarriage passed right over me.

I scrambled across the filthy dirt backyard, desperate to escape this nightmare. But my nearly paralyzed limbs could only get me so far. The vehicle finally broke free of what was left of Sonny's home and ground to a halt behind me. I heard the door open, followed by sadistic laughter.

Then a flashlight was shining in my eyes, and I heard a gun cocking. I knew my time on this planet was over.

"Jim, what the hell is wrong with you?" the killer said. I immediately recognized the voice, even though the glare of his flashlight blocked my view.

"Bradlee?" I said, stunned to find that our respected top cop was the killer.

"How the hell did you find her?" he said. "I buried her in that hole less than an hour ago."

"Didn't you see her ghost? She led me here."

He laughed like he was watching his favorite TV sitcom. "You were always so funny. Always had a great zinger or two that made my day."

"I had to find her. I loved her."

"Yeah, she was one fine-ass whore. One of my all-time favorites. I came up here every single night. But eventually ya get tired of their shit, even the hottest bitches. All that whinin' and cryin' gets on a man's nerves after a while. Tonight she finally wore out her welcome. Then you had to come along and ruin everything."

"I saw that you turned this into your own dungeon. How many other women have you brought up here?"

"I really liked you, boy. You worked hard, kept your nose clean, and gave me free pie and coffee whenever I stopped by. Why did you have to come messing up my good thing here?"

"How could you be such a freaking pig?"

He chuckled, the way my dad did before he hit me for being a smartass. Then he shot me in the arm.

"Dumbass move, boy. I was gonna make this easy on you, but now you're getting the whole nine yards."

Then he made a face. Anyone who has ever had the misfortune of seeing such an expression has been haunted by it ever since. The look of a heartless bully, someone so much bigger and stronger that they know you can't stop them from doing whatever they want to.

Of my four limbs, I only had one working arm. There was no way I could defend myself against this monster. He swaggered toward me, licking his lips. Then I saw him unzip, and my fear turned to cringing horror.

Until I saw the blade of a machete explode from his crotch. Someone from behind had forced a steel blade between his legs at his most delicate spot. He screamed in agony, his hands clutching at parts that weren't there anymore. They had dropped to the ground. As he fell to his knees, I saw Kaylee standing behind him, wielding the blade like a female warrior from an old Conan movie.

Bradlee tried to fire his pistol at me, but she swung down and sliced off his hand at the wrist. He rolled on the ground, sobbing like the spoiled little baby he was. We both believed he was finished, but he grabbed his side piece from under his pant leg and tried to fire. She buried the makeshift sword in his skull with a crunch. He rolled down an incline into a slimy ditch.

Sonny's cottage had finally had enough. The roof couldn't stand the strain. The entire place collapsed behind her.

Kaylee took two more steps in triumph, then fell next to me. We huddled together, both of us freezing from shock and barely breathing. She hugged me, and I kissed her cheek. She was my hero, and I was hers.

Eventually, she gathered enough strength to call in our emergency on Bradlee's police radio. We were whisked away to the nearest hospital. The bodies of seven other victims were found buried nearby. Enough other evidence was found at the scene of the crimes to make it an open-and-shut case against our former chief.

We rehabbed together, first at clinics, then at the gym. I had spinal cord damage that would likely give me problems the rest of my life. She had deep psychological scars which would probably never heal. But we fit together like two pieces of a jigsaw puzzle. There was a connection between us, an invisible bond. We could read each other's minds, hear each other's thoughts, finish each other's sentences. She could sense when a part of my body was causing me pain and massaged it away. I could tell when an unspeakable memory was haunting her and held her tight until the terrors receded into her subconscious.

We both quit our jobs, got married, and moved back to her hometown in Texas. We even started our own health club together. She runs the front register and takes care of customers. I run the back, handling the paperwork and the employees. She often hits the treadmills around closing time, when all you can see through the front windows is the darkness of the parking lot. A few times, as I gazed upon her gorgeous form, I could almost swear she was transparent. Just like that fateful night. Then I get these chills, and shake my head and check again, and she's as solid as the first day I met her back in school.

We both did extensive research, but we couldn't find any cases that were remotely close to what happened to us. Was she still alive, and did she rejuvenate when I unearthed her? Or was she dead, and did my caresses bring her back from the other side? Was she an astral image reaching out for me to help her or a ghost who returned when her body miraculously came back to life? Was it true love that brought her straight to me, or was it just her normal routine, and I just happened to be the first person to spot her?

Neither of us will ever know for sure. I also never figured out why the hell I woke up half naked that morning. I've never mentioned that part of the story to her. I'm trying to forget it myself.

Oh, and Sheriff Bradlee didn't die. Either Kaylee didn't have enough strength left to finish him off or she never wanted to kill him in the first place. I've asked her many times since then which it was, but she never answers. He's just brain damaged enough to be kind of helpless. He was sentenced to a state prison where the inmates just love cops.

Every single night.

Night Lights

Work had been a bitch lately. Three people had quit in the past two weeks, which left more work for the rest of us. And it wasn't like they were going to hire anyone new to help us. The new boss was all about the bottom line. One of those in-your-face screamers who were supposed to be extinct. A red-faced, jowl-shaking nightmare who had transferred from Memphis a few months earlier. And he had even less experience in what we did than the last clown. How could someone from food service know anything about telecom? Instead of driving the good employees like slaves, corporate should have been hiring middle managers who actually had a clue about what they were doing.

If you asked any normal human where they would want to spend the majority of their waking hours, it would be drinking margaritas on a beach or at a puppy farm saving strays from the streets, not at this rathole. And there were actual rats—and roaches, not to mention holes in the drywall that workers had punched or kicked in anger and frustration.

The place was illuminated by flickering fluorescent lights with exposed wiring, the transformers looking as if they were about to break loose and dive bomb our heads. The interior was painted a drab gray, the color of a rainy day that spoiled your birthday picnic. And don't get me started on the bathrooms. The ladies had not one, not two, but three plungers placed in strategic spots. Nothing says "gross" more than having to work down someone else's poop before doing your own business. The place was a nightmare.

But that morning was a ray of sunshine in an otherwise torrential week. I slinked around the snack machines, which blocked the view of my work area from the big guy's office window. Staying low, I wove through the rows of shabby cubicles until I reached my workstation. There, wrapped in a pretty blue bow, was a brand-new phone charger for my car. My cell phone and chargers had been stolen out of my drawer recently. In fact, a rash of thefts over the past few months had our already militant staff ready to revolt. It was bad enough we had to bust our asses for chump change. Having our personal property ripped off on top of that was grinding our gears.

Now some weirdo was probably hacking their way into all my personal data. Contacts, emails, photos of me and my friends and relatives, every text I'd sent or received for the past several years. Who deleted those until the little pop-up said they were out of storage room? I had to buy a brand-new phone the day before, and was still replacing all of my apps and getting it squared away. I didn't even have enough cash in my account to buy a new car charger. And here one appeared on my desk, as if a guardian angel had bought me a secret Santa gift in the middle of July. How did they know?

I meercatted around, neck stretched as high as possible, peering in every direction, trying to spot a happy face amongst the many miserable souls in their twisted antique headsets, looking as if they wanted to strangle whoever was on the other end of their calls. No one knows how terrible regular folks can be until they've worked retail or customer service. Or prostitution. But there were no smiles out there, just career zombies with expressions of deranged exasperation, realizing they had ten more hours of this bullshit till quitting time.

I got along well with all of them, except, of course, the person I had to sit next to. Arthur. A dweeb among dweebs. So nit-picky I'm shocked his parents didn't drop him off at the nearest orphanage by the time he hit kindergarten. He sat fidgeting on his swivel chair like a metronome, wearing the same ill-fitting Dungeons & Dragons T-shirt he sported every third day.

"Did you see who left me this gift?" I asked.

"Gift? You got a gift? Why didn't I get anything?" he whined, as if everyone had forgotten his sixteenth birthday.

He leapt past his partition and practically assaulted me, bellying up to my face as I sat at my desk, invading my personal space as I tried to scooch away. He ripped the present from my hands like a spoiled brat, examining the package as if it were some treasure he had to possess. How anyone could raise a child to be that rude without teaching them any common decency is one of the main reasons this country is so messed up. I had had enough of his bullshit.

"Gimme that," I said, ripping it out of his sweaty paws.

"Oh, you're so petty. You can't even let me look. I hope it's broken and has no warranty," he replied, acting as if his jealous behavior was all my fault.

I turned away and faced my monitor. There was no use arguing with clowns like him. He would be mumbling lame insults at me all day long, but I was used to that. And I didn't care, because someone somewhere in that hellhole cared about me enough to buy me that gift. I was so angry that the old charger connectors wouldn't connect with my new phone. I had eight of those suckers. And the kind for your vehicle are life savers when you forget to plug your phone in at home and drive away on an empty battery.

The rest of the morning was a typical blur of asinine callers and rude complaints. By lunchtime, Arthur had told everyone in the building who would listen that I had received a gift. The rumors had escalated, transformed as they leapt from mouth to mouth, the way gossip tends to do. Now it was a $1,200 iPhone, purchased for me by my wealthy sugar daddy, who I guess I had been humping in the rear parking lot for the past year. Even the cleaning ladies who didn't speak a word of English came strolling by searching for a glimpse of this wondrous freebie.

I didn't care. Truly happy moments don't come around very often anymore, so I've learned to treasure mine. That wondrous sensation acted like a force field, deflecting all the bad vibes, at least for the day.

Quitting time came so quickly, I actually clocked out a few minutes late. I never noticed the time flying by.

Wading through the lines of cars already beeping their way out of the parking lot, I waited until I got into my car to rip open the cardboard-and-plastic packaging. Eggs come in Styrofoam so flimsy that you have to check every time to see if any are broken, but these suckers are wrapped tighter than airport security. I kept a razor scraper in my glove compartment to peel off old city stickers from inside my windshield. They also came in handy for unexpected jobs like that one. I bent the container until the charger popped out. Then I plugged it in, and a little blue light appeared on top, proving it worked.

I smiled so hard, I almost started to cry. A stranger had bestowed upon me something that no one could purchase online or at any store. Kindheartedness. I was overwhelmed by the feeling of being liked, of being connected to another human being who thought I was special enough to treat to a gift. In these days of road rage and psychotic date rapists and living in the middle of millions of people yet feeling totally alone, it was more valuable than all the crypto in China.

Maybe it was all the months and years of living on my own and only having that dreaded snake pit of a company as an outlet for any type of intimacy that finally burst through. My eyes welled up so badly I had to pull over halfway home, so I could make it safely back to my apartment. A stupid grin invaded my face periodically for the rest of the day, remnants of that act of kindness.

Damn. I woke up in the middle of the night again. I looked out the window and saw the lonely darkness haunting me once more, the kind that almost spoke to me. Not a voice but a feeling, telling me that everyone else was still fast asleep, tucked away in their comfy blankets and dreaming happy thoughts while I felt wide awake and wanted to socialize with someone, so middle-of-the-day alert that I could hear the Great Dane fart in the apartment upstairs.

I checked my phone and saw it was 3:13 a.m. Great, just great. I always had to leave the house by 7:15, or I'd be late for work. What could I do to pass the time until then? Play video games? Scroll through memes and funny clips until it was time to hit the shower? That always ended badly. Dead tired by lunchtime. The afternoons dragged unmercifully. Each minute ticked along like an hour, as if one of those slave drummers on an ancient galley ship was pounding away in my head, and I was chained to my desk, rowing my life away, so some filthy rich corporate executive could buy a new condo in Barbados.

I needed to find something else to do that took a little exertion, so I could take a quick nap before my shower that would carry me through the day. The gym. It was open all night, and it was only seven minutes away. I could put in a quick workout and still get home with time to spare.

One of my favorite sensations was being able to leave the house not caring how I looked. Just some sweats, a sports jersey, and a ponytail. Toss on the old tennis shoes, grab my purse, phone, and keys and I was ready to go. None of the endless drudgery of make-up and hair styling and picking out which outfit I hadn't already worn that week that still fit during pre-period bloating. I was ecstatic to be going somewhere for some me-time with no chance of coworkers begging me for help on their projects or bosses bitching at me about deadlines.

I jogged down the steps and opened the glass security door that was so heavy against the wind that sometimes it almost wouldn't budge. I needed that extra shot of adrenaline and leg strength to power outside. It had to have been designed by men—ironically, to protect us girls from other men. The conundrums of living in such an archaic patriarchal society boggled the mind.

The chilly atmosphere sucked in and gave me a slap on the cheeks that I kind of enjoyed, welcoming me to another day. A few people close to me had passed away lately, causing a lot of tearful, mascara-smeared nights. They were like a couple of warning shots over my head about life in general. Tomorrow was promised to no one, except the assholes who didn't deserve it. It was a reminder to cherish every moment that destiny gave me.

The desolate blackness before dawn surrounded me, hiding the imperfections that only I noticed in the mirror. I bounced into my old faithful 2004 Corolla, the only thing in my life that I could count on. Yes, it needed a little maintenance occasionally, but it was always there when I needed it, and it never failed to take me where I needed to go, unlike every human I knew who was still breathing. I sped off, hoping that a little exercise was just what the doctor ordered.

Early morning traffic was such a joy. Just a few hours from then, those same dreamy, deserted roads I was taking to the gym will be bumper-to-bumper nightmares, with road-ragers honking and screaming and cutting each other off as if their lives and vehicles were meaningless to them. Nice people who would open the door at the gas station for you would also be the first ones to bulldoze you off the road if you weren't driving according to their own personal traffic rules. Anger replaced common sense and decency as soon as they got behind the wheel. But gliding down the streets that early was a breeze. I could even avoid the potholes that became unavoidable when road hogs overcrowded their lanes.

Then I noticed something from the corner of my eye: a small blue light in the passenger window. *Shit, is that the police?* I was speeding a little, but they usually let that slide late at night. They were too busy writing reports or eating donuts or napping to care. I tapped the brakes to slow down, but the red light from my rear tail lamps probably acted like a bullfighter's cape, igniting cop fury and urging them to charge after me.

But it wasn't the popo. To my relief, it was the reflection from the brand-new phone charger. It glowed when in use, so people wouldn't forget their phone was in the cupholder instead of in their purse. After I realized I was safe, I went right back to going ten miles per hour over the speed limit. I wanted to get there and back in time to relax for a while.

The light was kind of comforting. Blue has always been my favorite color. It was as if I had a little buddy to cruise around with. I'd get depressed being single after a certain while. They say being by yourself is so much better than being with the wrong person, but at least that person goes places and does things with you. Even my friends had become needy and greedy lately. Everything had to be about them. There was no time for me to express my feelings. As soon as I opened up about my inner self, they changed the subject to something that involved them. Empathy and a kind ear were becoming extinct faster than rhinos and tigers.

But then it started getting weird. As I drove, the reflection seemed to be changing, waving tiny sapphire arms at me. When I stopped at an intersection, I turned, and the movements ceased as well. Was I seeing things? Going crazy? When I started off slowly, the reflection remained docile, but when I hit the gas, it started moving again. I finally took my eyes off the road and flashed my vision onto the reflection.

It was smiling.

Like a freaky animated emoji flashing on my phone.

I swerved around a bit, glad I was the only vehicle on the road. But I mean, WTH, right?

I stopped for a red light, and it went right back to this emotionless blur. No sign of life. I sped up again and, boom! It was laughing and doing the wave like spectators at a football game. It swung its arms over its head, then dropped them. Then, after a short time, it waved them up again. I was freaking out.

I turned the corner, and there was the gym. I pulled into the lot and parked. My little pal had gone still once again. I realized I was trembling, partly because of the brisk air rushing in as I opened the door but also because of my psychotic break from reality.

I used the app on my phone to get into the gym, but nothing happened. I tried again, and it said I wasn't recognized. I figured the app wasn't synchronized with the gym doorway yet. I tried doing the email/password deal and clicked again. It said the app was still connecting with the service. My new phone had locked me out.

I was pissed. I could have stayed in my nice warm bed. This was bullshit. I got back in my car and drove off. As I did, I figured I could still get gas at the nearby station where it was cheaper than anyplace else. At least it wouldn't be a totally wasted trip. I zoomed the six blocks and pulled up to the pumps. I swiped my card repeatedly, but nothing happened. I looked at the video screen, and it said "Not In Service." I stepped back and saw all the pumps had the same notice. The fates were conspiring against me.

Now I was boiling over like soup in a microwave. I squealed out of the parking lot without even checking for oncoming traffic. What was I even living for? I had no guy in my life, no kids, and no close family or friends. My job was abysmal, my apartment should be condemned, and I was so allergic, I couldn't even have a puppy or a kitten. Why was I ever born? I sped down the street like a truck driver on crank. More tears. Why was I crying all the time lately? Because my life was such a tragedy that the government would declare it a national disaster. Who was I keeping myself alive for?

Just then I noticed my new little buddy. He was not only waving, he was also zooming around my passenger window like a video game avatar, begging for attention. Arms in the air like it just didn't care. Why would it be moving so much? Almost like it was trying to warn me of something.

Then my vision delved deeper through the glass. A semi was headed straight for me. There was no chance of avoiding it. This steel monster was going to turn me and my precious Corolla into gore-encrusted scrap metal.

Then I thought, why should I care? What was I trying to prove? That I was a trooper for trudging through my meaningless existence like a good little soldier? Maybe this was the best thing that could happen to me. It would look like an accident. My flimsy chain of acquaintances would show up at my wake, feigning sorrow, telling each other what a wonderful person I was, then forgetting I ever was a part of their lives the moment they walked out the door.

All of my hard work and heartaches would vanish in a heartbeat. I would finally be free. Funny how you can spend an entire day with barely a worthy thought crossing your mind, yet a million life-or-death scenarios can flash across the chasm of your mind in the brief instant before your demise. Screw it all. Y'all can kiss my ass goodbye.

No!

I was worth something. My life had a deeper meaning. My future was an undiscovered trove of wondrous events. All the brutal effort and romantic struggles were not going to go to waste. I was going to prove that my harshest critic—myself—had been wrong all along. This unbearable section of my life was just a segue to a dream world—husband, kids, career, or anything else I chose, and it would all be worthwhile.

I slammed on my brakes with both feet as hard as I had ever hit the leg press at the gym. I spun the steering wheel like a ship's captain in a terrible storm. My trusty auto swerved, and my bald tires squealed. The truck's horn wailed. Its headlights beamed down so brightly I was temporarily blinded. The impact was imminent. I said this poignant little prayer that I'll never remember.

The truck scraped the entire side of my car, taking off the mirror, then continued on its way like a mysterious ship to ports unknown. My entire body shivered as if I was being electrocuted, and I panted harder than I ever had, but my life was still my own. I had survived.

I turned to my little blue buddy. He was a little frightened. A drop of prismatic sweat dripped off the side of his face. But then he smiled and winked, giving me two thumbs up.

I'm not embarrassed to admit that I immediately slid over on my seat and kissed the glass right where his reflection was. Somehow, even though my body was blocking his reflection, he was still there. He blushed in an "aw shucks" kind of way. I wanted to hug him, but he was just an image on a piece of glass, which I was probably imagining. But whatever he was, he saved my life. I would have never noticed that truck if he hadn't been waving his butt off.

After the few moments of pure panic subsided, I got out and searched around outside. None of the parts left on the street were salvageable. I tossed the broken pieces in a trash can, so no one would get a flat, then I drove away.

As I crept along at twenty miles per hour, I realized my new charger also had a cigarette lighter attachment. After that mind-numbing terror, I could hotbox an entire pack of menthols. Reaching into my purse, I pulled out a smoke and fired it up. A crimson light reflected in the driver's window. I realized it was alive as well, in my mind at least. A little red character, as cute and sweet as my pal on the right.

He was funnier too. He made hilarious faces and did crazy things, like stretching his face like Silly Putty, so his eyes, nose, and smile were all distorted. He bounced up and down the window, stopping at the top, bottom, and sides and then rebounding back, like a character in an ancient video game that my grandpa had. After that horrible experience, I needed a laugh, and he was making me giggle as if I was ten years old. I was mesmerized, realizing what was going on around me but unable to react to it.

I never noticed that he had stolen my attention. I had taken my eyes off the road and wasn't paying attention to where I was going at all. His comic routine had entranced me. My vehicle was now a rudderless boat, drifting on an asphalt ocean. This guy was no angel. He was leading me astray. Hypnotized, I drove straight into a work zone, traveling high up an expressway ramp. I was headed toward some orange cones that signaled the end of the road. A thirty-foot drop to a side street was dead ahead.

Suddenly, my little blue savior went into action. He realized I was gazing in the other direction, so he found a way to cross over onto the windshield. He bopped up and down, waving, grew ten times his size, then shrank away again. I kind of noticed, but my mind was glued to the new red devil on my left.

In desperation, he zapped himself into my stereo system. Suddenly, that death metal station I avoided like the plague was playing full blast. The screaming singer and shrieking guitars shocked my eardrums and snapped me out of the trance. I saw the yawning chasm ahead, waiting to swallow my car.

There was no other way to prevent my death other than to slam into the concrete abutment to the right. I swerved into it, smashing my bumper, but I was alive. I turned and saw the red dude all bent out of shape. Little devil horns protruded from his head, and he was literally fuming, flames shooting out of his ears. He was so angry that I had saved my own life. I would never play the victim again. I rolled down my window, and he disappeared into the door.

Then I saw my little blue angel waving. He had returned to my right side, beaming with an ear-to-ear grin. He had saved my life not once but twice that night. Was he a figment of my overwrought delirium or a supernatural hero who appeared at the exact juncture in my life where I needed him most?

We drove home together. I didn't want to go inside. We played around like two old pals. I tried to catch him, but he zoomed around the car, zipping across every piece of glass, including the back window, even the one remaining mirror. I started to yawn, but I was having so much fun. My eyes began to droop, but I didn't notice. The sun crept over the horizon, but I never wanted the game to end.

"Hey. Wake up. You drunk again?"

An unnecessarily hard pounding on my window woke me out of my stupor. The neighbor lady from my building was heading to her job and saw me sleeping out in the parking lot. I checked the time. I was way late. Then I checked my charger light. Just a reflection. No signs of life. Had it all been a crazy dream?

With no chance to think about it, I raced around trying to make myself presentable enough to make it through the day without someone asking if I had gotten laid the night before. My little blue buddy seemed bummed out as I got out of my car. His sad puppy dog eyes begged me to stay. So, I did the next best thing and brought him with me. At least he wouldn't be alone out there all day.

I still felt like I had that "walk of shame" look as I entered the office, but there was nothing I could do about it. I punched in late, so everyone got a chance to ogle at my appearance as I strolled to my desk. Women glared at me with that half-envious, half-resentful look reserved for the slut of the day. Guys had that "oh baby" sparkle in their eyes, each hoping their smile would attract me enough to ask them out.

As I passed by Arthur, he dropped his jaw like a cartoon wolf. "Whoa, look at you! Did your sugar daddy keep you up all night?"

I tapped the leg of his chair on my way past. As he was already off balance from squirming on his seat, he fell like a drunken jackass onto the filthy floor. The entire section burst into uncontrollable laughter as he stumbled to his feet, whining, his headset earplug shoved halfway up his nostril.

Arthur ran off to complain to the boss, but I didn't give a shit. I wasn't in the mood for any of them. Except one. How would I ever figure out who had given me such a wonderful gift? Whoever it was, I could never thank them enough. They were my reason for being. I had grown up a lot overnight. My attitude was a mirror opposite of what it had been the day before.

Instead of complaining about all the things I didn't have, I figured it was time to start being happy about what I did have. It's so freaky how the mind can turn into quicksand without us realizing it. Every little disappointment makes us sink deeper and deeper into depression. Some people never figure it out, never dig their way back out of that trap.

But I did. I was in a rut, but I was going to make sure I was happy about every good thing that happened in my life. A tasty cup of coffee, an onion ring in my French fries, a smile from a stranger. I would concentrate on anything that could bring joy to my life. I wasn't allergic to birds. Maybe a spazzy little cockatiel would make me happy. I also vowed to find a better job and a nicer apartment in a town that wasn't such a downer.

I placed my treasured car charger on my desk and prepared to start my day. I was never going to let it out of my sight again.

"Hey, how did my present work out for you?" a voice asked from behind me. I whirled about and saw it was the new guy. I hadn't caught his name. He was around five foot ten inches tall—six feet in guy measurements. He had curly dark brown hair, a shiny smile, and the cutest dimples. A fixer-upper for sure but not one I'd want to flip right away.

He had that trustworthy vibe. Everyone has a few red flags, but he kept his under control. A little heavy on the cologne, but he knew he had known he was going to approach me that morning, and he wanted to make a good first impression. Overanxious. That meant he wasn't thinking about me as a hit-and-run. He was interested in dating me. A "boyfriend and girlfriend going out to dinner and the movies" type of relationship. I melted a little. He had seen me roll in like last night's stale pizza, yet he had still approached me with romantic intentions. Color me impressed.

"That was you? Oh my God, thanks so much. How did you know?"

"I overheard people talking in the break room. I saw you the day I started, and well, I thought you were kinda cute. I was wondering if you wanted to hang sometime."

Mike. His name was Michael. I haven't decided which I like better yet. He's not a knight in shining armor, but he does drive a freaking hot 1,000 cc Kawasaki Ninja. We go riding all the time now. Hanging tight onto his abs while we cruise everywhere has just expanded my senses. The smells and sounds of the open road are like a breath of fresh air for my psyche. We laugh and make love and watch movies all night, throwing popcorn at each other.

We pooled our cash together and opened a food truck, selling wood-fired pizzas on weekends at all the nearby fests and sports events. We also found a pretty cottage to rent with a garage large enough to hold the truck and his bike. My faithful car gets parked on the street out front but not for long. We plan to buy a minivan soon because he wants to have kids.

Sadly, the day our eyes locked for the first time was the last time I ever saw my little blue buddy. When we went out for lunch, someone stole my charger off my desk. I should be getting him back soon, though— after my evil ass boss goes on trial for theft. He got into a horrible car accident recently and has been stuck in the hospital for months rehabilitating. Funny, but they found a bunch of the items stolen from employees' desks in his trunk. My charger was plugged into his dashboard at the time of his crash. I wonder if that little red devil had anything to do with the accident.

My boss doesn't work there anymore, and pretty soon, if the food truck keeps doing as well as it has, I won't be either.

Morning Jog

My name is Eddie Warden. I'm an independent investment advisor. Very independent. Okay, so I'm a con man. Work up and down the East Coast getting new suckers hooked on all the hottest new trends. Ponzi schemes, penny stock swindles, rare coins that aren't really that rare. Lately I've been huge with crypto, NFT's, Ecash. Suckers hear wild stories about people making millions on pennies and they all want in. But they're too dumb or lazy to figure out how these things work. They want all the profits without doing any of the homework. Easy targets.

That's where I come in. I give them this vague pitch about these newest non-fungibles that are about to be bigger than Bitcoin. Hit them with "Little to no risk for the investor" and other bullshit to put them at ease. Show them brochures and a fancy fake website that supposedly explains everything. You should see the thirsty expressions in their eyes. That beautiful combination of greediness and stupidity that every grifter is searching for. Lambs just begging to be fleeced.

Of course, these scams don't work with everyone. After specializing in swindles like this for a few years, I can pretty much tell when I get a chump hooked. Sometimes I can barely keep my cool because I can tell they're itching to sign on that dotted line. They invariably waver because it's so hard for them to comprehend what I'm saying. Until I tell them how these things are ready to explode, and they must buy immediately, or it will be too late. Then just reel them in.

It's kind of like yelling at some hot babe while you're driving past her. Nine out of ten times they'll ignore you or flip you the bird. I've even had one crazy bitch take a shot at me. But there's always gonna be that one who smiles and waves back. The exhilaration forces a shit-eating grin across your face. You pull a U-turn knowing she'll be getting the back seat of your car all sticky by the end of the night.

Of course, once I glom up a healthy chunk of their finances, I close up shop before the feds start an investigation. If you keep your illegal operations under a certain amount, it's not worth their trouble. Just don't make a pig of yourself and they'll let it all slide. The whole mess is chalked up to bad luck and a bull market. The clients cry. Boohoo. Tough shit.

A few have come after me, threatened my life. Pointed their guns at me and demanded their cash back. But I've always been able to talk my way out of it. Planning revenge is so easy, but actually pulling the trigger is way tougher than you'd think. There's always a way to calm them down, channel their anger away before they open fire. I always say that I saw them drive up and already called 911. The cops are halfway here by now. Think of your family. You'll be stuck in prison for the rest of your life, never seeing them again, and you still won't have your money back. It's such an adrenaline rush to cheat death over and over again.

It also helps that I'm also a world class marathon runner. New York, Boston, Chicago, even the Bahamas. Won races all over the country. My trophy case is massive. People on the circuit all know me. They stop me in the street like I'm a superstar athlete. I've had to crawl out of the back windows of quite a few seedy motels, racing off on foot for miles and miles to avoid whatever trouble was banging at my door.

But that's just how I pay the bills for my true mission in life. Some people want to become cops and protect the public. Some want to become ministers and preach to the masses. My calling is not that noble. It's finding sexy women on the internet. And not for that long term relationship crap either. As soon as bitches get too clingy, I cut them loose. Give them a Tinder-ectomy. I'm into hit and runs. Pump and dumps. I tell them what I'm all about up front. They know the score and get just as much from me as I get from them. Maybe more.

Been Skyping with two of the hottest bitches I have ever seen the past few days. Ginnie and Lynnie. They say they're twin sisters, but they don't look quite the same. Some features are kind of different, but who the fuck cares. I've had identical twins before and it's like banging clones. I was tripping on something, and they freaked me out. When we were twisted up together under the blankets, I couldn't tell where one started and the other one ended. A few deviations make them more interesting.

Got totally wasted last Wednesday night, ended up swiping through the casual sex sites and *dayum!* Nearly dropped my phone. Hooked up with them on video and have been chatting ever since. Turned the filters off and they still looked like a pair of wet dreams. And they weren't talking about dating and love and all that. Chicks who get their hearts involved end up getting them broken. It's nothing personal. If they were looking for husbands, they were on the wrong app.

I stripped down to my boxers and let them check out my body. I hit free weights at the gym and make sure my abs are six-packed. Must have liked what they saw, because the things they said they wanted to do to me made me want to knock one off while they were still on the phone. Set up plans to drive down on Friday after work. They booked us a room at the Necron Hotel, just northeast of Savannah, Georgia.

I've been squatting at this vacant condo in Manhattan, so that's a crazy long drive. But if we even did half the stuff they mentioned, it would be way worth it. Got anxious and took the day off. Left early, jumped in my black Lexus LC500 and made it through the Lincoln Tunnel from Midtown in record time. Got off onto I-95 at Secaucus and was on my way. Call it luck, call it Karma, but traffic was practically non-existent. I was flying, hitting 90 mph when my fuzz buster wasn't beeping off. If I didn't stop for gas and coffee, I could have made it in ten hours, tops.

My little guy jumped in anticipation as I hit the Georgia state line. Couldn't wait to sweat up the sheets with those two. Weaved through traffic like a fighter pilot skying between the clouds. Savannah mileage signs got smaller and smaller. Texted them to say I was almost there. Got a weird text back from them. Bizarre symbols I had never seen on a phone before. Must have been a screw-up with the signal. These burner phones sometimes have glitches.

But just as I was closing in for the kill, the jams in my ride started flaking out. The streaming service got cut off by some tragic-sounding country music station. Hate that trash. I hear one twang at a party and I'm out of there.

Then a strange mist hit. It came out of nowhere, a thick yellowish fog. Got my windshield so oily I could hardly see the road. Had to keep hitting the window washer to cut through the grease. Pissed me off, I had to close the convertible roof. Hit he hazards and drove on the shoulder, just barely tapping the accelerator to move forward. Kept running over those warning indentations in the concrete that rattle your tires so sleepy truckers don't kill themselves.

WTF, this sucked. Squinted to see the lines on the pavement. Worried some asshole was gonna slam into me from behind. End up in one of those forty car pileups that happen in winter when the roads get icy. What the hell was this smoky shit? Did some old factory burn down nearby? I tried to turn the dial and get the news, but all I got was hillbilly trash so ancient that even Johnny Cash would turn it off. Checked my phone real quick so I didn't run off the road, but the entire screen was filled with those whacked out symbols.

My little head was against it, but my big head made the decision to stop completely, until I spotted a strange exit through the haze. Didn't look like a regular interstate off ramp. More like a gravel turnoff onto some farmer's land. But I didn't want my baby getting dented, so I steered off onto the pathway. It was actually easier to follow, because there were tall bushes lining either side. Figured maybe the owner of this redneck plantation might have a landline that worked. There was a slight incline, and I was about to stop again. But it seemed as if the fumes were starting to clear up.

Excited, I went a little faster. Then there was a steep dip in the road. Almost like driving off a cliff. My car rolled faster and faster. I hit the brakes, but they skidded out on the gravel. I heard a horrible sound. Something snapped in my front axle. Maybe I hit a pothole or ran over a goat, I don't know. But it was a deal-breaker. I hit the brakes, hoping the smog would pass. Opened the window to check it out, but it smelled even more rancid, like my old frat house after an all-night sorority mixer. I immediately began coughing like I had COPD. Started getting sleepy all of a sudden. Played around with the radio and swiped on my phone until I guess I passed out.

Woke up feeling like something was lifting my car off the ground. My guts churned as I opened my eyes, fearing the worst. Early daylight glittered through the trees, and the fog had vanished. Looked misty, as if the morning dew hadn't evaporated yet. Time on my phone said 6:37 A.M. And a tow truck was pulling my beautiful baby by an automatic chain onto its rear flat top. I opened the window and yelled, but the noise of the machinery blocked me out. The chains locked tight, and the driver took off with me still in the car.

I was swearing at the dude as loud as I could, but he refused to stop. We did pass by some really amazing scenery. The area was truly beautiful, with that smoky mist highlighting the dawn sunshine. I felt a lot better when the gravel road transformed into slick asphalt. We passed a long forest of weeping willow trees, and then, right before me, was a state-of-the-art hotel. I mean this sucker was sweeter than the new luxury resort in the Hamptons. Right in front was a huge sign that said "Necron Hotel".

I was shocked. Somehow, I ended up right where I was supposed to. Never heard of this chain before. Definitely wasn't the Marriott. Maybe they were a Georgia thing. I didn't care. Still worried about my car, but at least I wasn't lost anymore. Lynnie and Ginnie, here I come.

When we stopped in front, the driver came around. I was expecting a regular Gomer, with buck teeth, floppy ears, oil-stained overalls and a backwards baseball cap. But this guy was handsome, almost looked like a model, dressed as if he were headed to church. I got out to give him some attitude, but he cut me off.

"Listen, you looked comfy back there, and you were caught on a scary embankment. It was safer for you to stay in your car than to fall off into the ravine."

"I guess that's okay. What's the damage look like? I heard a snap." I asked.

"No damage I can see. Might be your shocks. I'll bring her in next door and check her out."

"Great. I'll be checking into this hotel for the weekend. I'll call you with my info. Have her ready by Sunday night."

"Will do," he said, and pulled away around the corner towards a service station right down the block.

I turned around and strolled down the opulent walkway towards the front doors. Gorgeous Olympic-sized swimming pool. Tennis courts. One of the guys playing seemed familiar. Think I watched him playing at the U.S. Open in Flushing. The chick teeing off on the golf course also looked semi-famous. Pretty sure I saw her on one of those swimsuit editions. Walked inside the crystal-clear glass front doors to find they even had a casino. I thought there was only one in the whole state? I spotted at least one wise guy from Manhattan at the craps table. This place was like a haven for minor celebs. I fit right in.

It was crazy, but those strange symbols I had seen on my phone were all over the walls. Must be corporate logos or something. Entered the dome that held the registration and concierge service desks. Kind of creepy to see the whole hall nearly empty, but then again, it wasn't like we were in downtown Atlanta. I approached the front counter and the sweet young babe working looked me over like a piece of meat. She smiled as if she was expecting me.

"Mr. Warden?" she asked, guessing who I was. "Ginnie and Lynnie were worried about you. We're so happy you're alright."

"You know those two?"

"Oh, yes, we're really close friends. They told me to tell you to go up to room 333, they'll meet you there this afternoon."

"Okay, where do I sign in?"

"That's all been taken care of, sir."

"Maybe you can meet us up there for a drink after your shift? I mean, since you're such tight friends," I said with a smirk.

"Go get some rest," she laughed. "You're going to need it."

Well, I was hoping to be waist-deep in twins by now, but at least I wasn't still mired in that smog in the middle of nowhere. I took the elevator up, checking myself out in the mirrors. The sudden lift and quick rising speed made me a bit lightheaded.

I kind of stumbled down the hall. Guess the bizarre designs in the hotel carpeting made me a little dizzy, with all those strange geometric shapes and weird color combinations. Stopped at room #333, and noticed it was an adjoining suite. #333B was right next door. Twin rooms for twin girls. Hope that desk clerk does show up. I brought my three favorite drugs; Viagra, Cialis, and Levitra, so I was ready for anything.

Opened the door, and damn, it looked like a mobster's penthouse in Vegas. Foyer, full bar, TV practically the size of a theater movie screen. Thick mosaic pillars, arched ceilings, plush furniture. Beds so huge you have to leave breadcrumbs to find your way back to your partner. If this is what Georgia is like, I'm moving down immediately.

I did the running backwards plop onto the bed. Judges would have given me a 9.8 for style and difficulty. A complimentary candy popped up off the pillow and landed on my chest. Loved these things. Had more of those symbols on the wrapper. I let it melt on my tongue. It was a dark chocolate with some wild extra flavor. Hazelnut? Maybe, who cares? It was delicious. Flicked on the tube, and it went straight to porn. Got into it for a minute, but then I thought, what am I watching this for? Gonna have the real thing knocking at my door in a few hours.

I turned to the nightstand and noticed one of those old Magic Fingers Mattress Massager things. Free for all guests of the hotel. I guess they don't take quarters anymore. Who the hell carries change around nowadays? Just turn it on and it would vibrate for a few minutes. Kind of tacky for a fancy place like this, but why not? I pressed the button, and it started up. Felt so good, my eyes shut, and my jaw dropped.

Whoever designed this thing was a genius. Those old ones just rumbled like the bedsprings were shaking. This was exquisite. I mean, it almost felt like these individual fingers were caressing each muscle and treating it like a Swedish masseuse. Every knot in my body began to unwind. Every tendon, every ligament, every strand of cartilage loosened up. It was as if my entire framework started to detach. I'd never felt anything like it.

My mind soared like I was tripping on something. When the machine stopped, I figured I would fall right asleep, but instead, I was invigorated. Had all this pent-up energy pumping inside of me. Changed the station and found that channel which shows all the hotel amenities. Had a commercial. Said they had the finest running course in Southern Georgia. Perfect for a slow jog or a marathon race. The video made it look so amazing. The curtains were drawn open, and the weather looked awesome.

I was overexcited, and I didn't want to pop too soon on the lovely ladies. So, I put on some shorts and a t-shirt and headed downstairs. The back entrance had arrows leading to the course. I was so anxious I almost started jogging inside the building. Once I got out there, I noticed the commercial didn't lie. It truly was a nice runway. Brand new. So, I started off, happy as hell. I figured, jog a few miles, take off a little pressure, then shit, shower, shave. I'd be primed and ready for action.

It started out with that green rubber track material. Softer on the soles. Really started moving out there, faster than usual. Had a full head of steam as I passed behind the back of the parking lot. Further on, nature took over. The trees and flowers and stuff were just stunning. Breathing in was a pleasure. Clean, fresh air with a fragrant, outdoorsy scent. Nothing like New York's infamous pollution. That was like sucking straight from a taxi exhaust pipe. I raced along with little to no effort, feeling like an Olympic Champion. My speed was off the charts. I ran track in high school, but never remembered having this much velocity. I hit a higher gear I never knew I had. Almost being forced along faster than possible.

Up and down hills, around curves, through epic forest areas. I glided along with a smile, no huffing or puffing. I spotted all types of wildlife. Birds flying overhead. Raccoons and opossums squirreling around the trees. Coyotes, rabbits, even a bobcat in the distance.

Then a regal deer, a white tail with ten prongs, sprinted alongside me as I ran. Somehow, I could almost keep up with him. The feeling was tremendous. Like I was one with Mother Nature. He stopped at a guardrail. I turned and he watched me keep racing up an incline. I could swear it was almost smiling. But it felt as if I had beaten him. I was king of the forest.

Then I reached the crest of a knoll, and the bottom practically fell out of the racecourse. I had to run so fast that I couldn't stop. This downhill was so steep, it took me along for a ride. Fear swept through my entire being. It was like racing down a cliff. My feet kept pumping, but it was all too crazy. My shins started to ache as if I had terrible splints.

All of a sudden, my foot twisted under my ankle. I knew this was a bad sprain, maybe a fracture, but I had no choice but to keep right on going.

Then things started snapping, making louder noises than my car did. My joints popped. Knees buckled. My legs felt as if they were going to detach from my pelvis. One by one, my tendons and ligaments started to rupture.

Suddenly, my right foot snapped right off. I left it behind me on the road as I stomped along on the stump. Then my other foot broke away. I couldn't stop running until finally my ankle broke off at the knee. I tumbled to the pavement, rolling viciously down the mountainside. Fingers flew off my hands as I braced for my fall. My left arm cracked away. Right leg separated from my hip.

Then my head hit the turf and bounced loose from my neck. It rolled down and settled in the ravine, spinning like a top, followed by the rest of my body parts.

I couldn't believe what was happening. This felt as if I were in some surrealistic European art film. The freakiest part was that it wasn't bloody or messy. It was as if I were a doll, and the parts simply dislodged.

I lied there for a while. It seemed like hours, but it may have been simply moments. I don't think time flows for a discombobulated body like it does for normal people. My head had rested on its side, and all I could see was a small woodsy pathway. Up walked Ginnie and Lynnie. My gorgeous playmates. Looking so sexy in their tiny shorts and halter tops. They smiled so sweetly at me.

I was beyond common sense. The reality I once took for granted was now a distant dream floating away up into the mountains. Existence for me had zigzagged into some warped, PCP-induced nightmare. I felt my innards deforming themselves inside, contorting as if by magic. The ecstatic excitement I had felt, anticipating hooking up with these freakishly hot women, now transformed into a morbid despondency.

I wasn't angry at the girls or screaming in pain. I was simply lying there, wondering what was to become of me now.

I watched helplessly as they gathered up my parts one by one, tossing them into a wheelbarrow like tinder for a fireplace. My head went last, rolling around on top of my mangled corpse. Or is it really a corpse if I'm still alive to see it? I don't know, that's something the living would have to decide. I was in some hazy gray area. Almost alive but mostly deceased.

As they pushed me along, I could see a strange town. It wasn't new and bright and beautiful like the hotel. It was old and creaky, yet with a charm all its own. The framework of the tumble-down shacks was irregular, built strangely. Windows off-kilter, porches crafted in oblique, enigmatic angles. As if the entire village had been nailed together by inbred maniacs.

Out of it stumbled its strange residents. Odd people, I thought. Beautiful but warped somehow. Perfect in their macabre imperfection.

They set me down in the village square. A tall hunk of a man wandered up carrying a massive old book. Its cover had the face of a demon carved into it, surrounded by those weird symbols. He opened it on a page marked with a blood red sash. Started chanting a bizarre hymn. Words I'd never heard in my life. Or perhaps my hearing and comprehension had been distorted by what they had done to me.

The townsfolk gathered around, as if they were celebrating some kind of religious ceremony. But this wasn't any Evangelical faith, like those infomercials asking for donations in the middle of the night. It was malevolent. Evil. A secret cult of demon worshippers. Ginnie and Lynnie stood on either side and serenaded me like gospel singers from Hell.

76

The rest of the bizarre inhabitants joined in. A haunting chorus which made my body parts quiver in fear. It seemed like they were all products of generations of incest, malformed, or just not right somehow. Twisted faces. Mangled limbs. Hunchbacks, paraplegics. Crutch and wheelchair folks. Some of them didn't even look human. Almost like sick creatures from a cheapo horror flick. They looked down at me with glee. I wondered why I made them so happy.

Then they attacked, grabbed at my parts as if I was on sale at Walmart on Black Friday. I noticed they were all taking pieces of me that they needed. A thumb. An ear. A big toe. They held them to the corresponding spots, and each appendage mysteriously attached to their bodies. Children who had mangled legs grabbed mine. They held them tightly to the joint near the hip. I watched as they shrank down to exactly the right size, then the skin remolded to fit perfectly onto their bodies. A guy with no left arm snatched up mine. I felt one of my organs ripped from my innards. I think it was my liver. A pretty yet ghoulish woman placed it at her abdomen. It was absorbed right through her flesh, a satanic transplant.

Ginnie and Lynnie grinned down on me like sexy little demons. I saw barely visible scars around their necks. They had been through this before. And as they dug their hands into my chest, for the first time in my life, I felt those warm, romantic emotions they write songs about. I realized my heart now belonged to them.

A Bloody Little Christmas

*I*t was the stuff that nightmares were made of.

My beautiful seventeen-year-old daughter was just a few desperate yards out of my reach, being drained of life by an undead creature, and I could do nothing to save her.

I struggled toward her on my chest through the ankle-deep snow, which crept inside my ugly Christmas sweater through the open collar, freezing my skin. I strained as hard as I could, digging my fractured fingernails into the icy black tar roof, dragging myself forward. But I could barely make out their writhing, shadowy forms through the darkness and heavy snowfall. My vision was blurred by blood oozing down from a gaping wound in my skull. My head was pounding, and my mind was swirling in a daze from the severe blow I had just received while trying to protect her.

It was the middle of the night on Christmas Eve. I had just been awoken from a deep, peaceful sleep and then been dealt a possible concussion. Could all of this be some kind of strikingly realistic dream? How else could I explain a supernatural being kidnapping my only child?

I hated winter. The older I got, the farther south I wanted to move, the more tropical the better. As a kid I hated the sweaty heat of summer and loved the cold and snow. But working outdoors for over twenty years twisted that around to the polar opposite.

My daughter loved the idea. When the wife and I took her to Disney World, the humidity curled her normally straighter-than-straight hair just the way she'd always dreamed of. She took one peek in the mirror, and her lips curved into a confident smile. Rebecca had always been so tall that the boys kept their distance, afraid to be spotted with a schoolgirl who was bigger than they were. She told her mother that her long midsection was so perfect for a bikini that guys down there would overlook her height issues—the type of thing a daughter never shares with her dad.

I was never one of those overprotective morons who try to prevent their daughters from growing up. She was almost an adult now, and I wanted her to find a guy who would make her happy forever, to love her the way her mom loved me.

With just one more year until her graduation, we decided to move to the Gainesville area, so she could attend college for a medical degree. Becca would live on campus, and I would rent a place nearby, though not so close that it would seem like I was spying on her. She was a great kid, and I never thought I would need to be an overbearing father who dictated her every move.

That was until she started candy-striping at the local hospital. I guess they don't want people to call it that anymore. It's volunteering, but it's basically the same thing. She assisted the nurses and doctors with menial chores that they had neither the time nor inclination to do. I guess volunteers don't empty bedpans any more either, but they assist the staff with pushing wheelchair patients around and getting them ice or something to read. As if the mega-corporations who run our hospitals couldn't afford to pay someone to do that. They charge thirty dollars for a damn Aspirin and as much as five hundred for an IV bag that only costs them a buck. More one-percenters raking it in while never compensating the girls who provide the slave labor.

Working there gave Becca valuable experience and looked good on her university applications. I was so proud of her. The kid spent all day at school, did her homework, and still made it on time every day she was scheduled to work. She never complained, even though all of her friends got to run around partying and doing who knows what else.

I never told her the stories, but I was one of those wild punks. Sex, drugs, and rock 'n' roll, not to mention rap and a little country. But she probably figured it out when some of my old buddies stopped over for parties and blabbed on and on about how crazy I used to be.

I scabbed out. My parents had connections with the local politicians and got me a city job with the streets and sanitation department. Union work with great insurance, a pension, paid vacations, the whole nine yards. If not for that, I don't know where I'd be. Probably where my old pals are: spending every nickel and dime they make at scrub jobs at the worst dive bars they could stumble home from. But I never acted all high and mighty. I realized how lucky I was, and I never looked down on or made fun of those less fortunate dudes, who I still hung with.

Becca was the same way. She treated everyone she met with the same kindness and respect, whether it was the principal or the lady who scrubbed the toilets. I like to think that came from me, but my wife was even kinder. We would all still be one happy family if it wasn't for the big "C." Everyone thinks divorce is the main cause of families breaking up, but cancer has to be right up there. I miss Dawn so much, but at least I have Becca here to remind me every day of how wonderful she was. At first their similarities bothered me, but now they're a comfort and a joy.

Once Dawn passed three years back, things began to change. Becca withdrew and became moody. She even talked back to me, which she had never done before. I thought it was all part of maturing from a kid into a teenager, but a part of it had to stem from her mom's death. Both events slammed into her at the same time, a double whammy of painful loss and social anxieties that pummeled her from every side. Divorce might have been a kinder fate.

I thought I had been doing a decent job of raising her alone until Anton entered the picture. Becca met the cretin at the hospital. He was an orderly on the night shift who kept "accidentally" running into her as he was coming in, and she was leaving. It was the same old trick I used on Dawn when we were both working at McDonalds. She finally caved, and we started dating. That's what was happening with Becca and Anton.

Something about him didn't feel right, and it went way beyond a dad safeguarding his little girl. He was one of those pasty-faced Goths who thought he was better and smarter than anyone else, all makeup and piercings and black leather and silver studs. He would have fit right in when I was in school back in the early eighties.

I tried not to be judgmental, but he was the living embodiment of fingernails scraping across a blackboard. He had nasty yellow teeth, and his canines were extra long and pointy, almost like fangs. I put up with this clown for the sake of my kid, but I spent most of my time sitting on my hands to prevent myself from smacking him.

He kept trying to convince me that he was only nineteen, but he looked twenty-four and acted like he was older than dirt. And he knew stuff that punks his age would have no interest in, like old movie stars from the thirties and forties. He would spout out all these trivial facts about celebrities I had barely heard of, and he knew the dialogue from *Casablanca* like I knew the words to *Die Hard*. Both flicks were way before his time.

Dawn and I got married not long after our Big Mac careers ended. There was no way I was gonna let that happen with these two. I was kind of a wild man, but this guy was a creep. I hated him from the moment I laid eyes on him.

He was taller, better built, and better looking than me. Strike one.

He had no parents, friends, or relatives living in the area. Strike two.

He never wanted to go out for lunch, watch a ballgame, or do anything else during the day. Said he had a skin condition that was worsened by sunshine. Huge strike three.

I played it cool, realizing that within six months, her senior year would be over, and we would be moving to Florida. No way this Lurch was going to survive in the Sunshine State. Becca told me she still agreed with the plan, that Anton was just a tweener, someone to spend time with until Mr. Right came along.

But then things started to change. Becca became colder and more distant, spending all her time with that stiff. If she had worked in the morgue, she would have noticed the corpses had more life than Anton did. Then he started with the dictator bullshit, telling her what to do, what to eat, and how to dress. Huge red flags for narcissistic behavior.

Those were the final straws. I told them both I was ending it. They couldn't see each other anymore under any circumstances. I knew it was a bad time, right before the holidays. Girls always want to have a guy around that time to take to parties and show everyone that they have a boyfriend. Most dudes only go to those parties to see which of her friends and cousins and hot aunts they can hit on later.

It was a horrible move on my part. Adolescence, her mom dying, and now her dad slapping her with ultimatums. It was strike three. Becca started staying over at his place more and more. After a few weeks, she began to look so weak and drained that I thought he had gotten her hooked on something. I worried about her as December's frosty nights rolled in. I lost so much sleep staring out the bedroom window, praying she would come home safe. What could I do? The harder I tried to break them up, the stronger his grip on her became.

One morning she strolled in to pick up some snacks, clean clothes, and a new toothbrush, as if my condo was the local Target or something. I couldn't stop thinking that those ancient parents who chained daughters to their bedposts had the right idea, but I had to play it cool.

"So, when's the next time I'll see you?" I asked.

"I'll be home for Christmas," she sang with a snarky tone as she marched out the door.

Becca didn't realize it, but she was breaking my heart. She was too busy trying to please the new man in her life. It's so weird how a perfectly sensible person can meet some random new dirtbag and never notice what a terrible influence they are, unwittingly destroying one of the closest relationships they will ever have.

Our arguments at home turned into texting battles over the phone. Becca finally defeated me by changing numbers. She took his side in every dispute and began dropping hints that Florida was out of the picture.

This was not good. Not only was I losing my baby, she was jeopardizing her entire future. She was tossing all those years of hard work, perfect attendance, and straight A's out the window for this loser she had just met. I had to stop this, to save her from herself.

It all came to a boil on Christmas Eve. Becca wanted to spend it with Anton, even though we had gone to see our relatives at my parents' house every year since she was born. I told her no, and that was final. She cried and pleaded for me to let her go, acting like a spoiled princess who couldn't get her way. So, I told her neither of us were going anywhere. We were both staying home where I could keep an eye on her. If we went to the family party, she was a flight risk. She could say she was going to the bathroom and then run out the nearest exit.

Becca ignored me and made a beeline for the door. I grabbed her arm and held her back. She was furious and stormed around the place, crying and bitching like a caged animal. She kicked a hole into our inflatable Santa Claus. He popped and slowly sank into a sad pile of vinyl onto the floor. She ripped all the lights down from the ceiling. Then she swiped all the decorations off the buffet, including our favorite Christmas glasses, the ones Dawn had engraved with all three of our names on them. They crashed to the floor into a million unretrievable shards.

I'm not an emotional guy; I cry maybe once a decade, but Bezza seized up, realizing she had committed something heinous. She looked up at me with that little girl face again, but this was my old Becca, the true version. Her eyes welled up, as did mine. Those were her mom's most precious possessions, ones she wrapped and packed away so delicately every year you would think they were Fabergé eggs. And now they were gone forever.

Something snapped in Becca at that moment. But in a good way. A wonderful way. Now it was clear to her that she had been ensnared into some kind of cultish funk. Anton had seized control of everything in her mind that made her special and hid those things away, like holiday decorations crammed into the back corner of the attic. The crash of the crystal released her spirit from the lonely cell in which he had imprisoned it.

"Oh my god, Daddy. I am so sorry," she cried out with all the emotions that had been trapped inside her since that devil had taken command.

Just as we closed in for an "all is forgiven" hug, someone pounding on the door broke up our tender moment. We both knew who it was. Becca shrank back, afraid of what he might do, but I wasn't afraid of that young shit.

Although now I know I should have been.

"Anton, you are no longer—"

Before I could finish my ultimatum, he blasted through the door like it was made of balsa wood. Shards flew everywhere, and the knob bounced across the floor and spun like a dreidel, coming to a halt twenty feet away. He waltzed in with all the bravado of a villain in one of those blockbuster superhero flicks.

And rightfully so. I was shocked to see that Anton had evolved into a completely different person, a larger-than-life character. He had gone from an emo freak to a commanding presence. His face was glowing, as pale as the full moon. His twisted eyes blazed red in the Christmas tree lights. His canines protruded from his lips as if he were a rabid wolf on the prowl.

As intimidated as I felt, the primitive need to protect my daughter revved my engines. I swung my best haymaker at his smug mug, but he ducked it easily, laughing at my feeble attempt.

"You can't keep me from her, geezer. Your life will come to an abrupt halt tonight, but your daughter's immortality is about to begin."

I tried to grab Anton in a headlock, but he backhanded me to the floor like a punk-ass kid. Then he grabbed Becca and bared his teeth. They were full-fledged fangs, twice as long as before, the points as sharp as needles. He clutched her to his chest and was about to bite her. I couldn't believe it. He was an actual vampire.

I wiped the taste of floor from my mouth and snatched up a hefty spike of wood from the shattered door lying nearby. Launched toward him from behind, I stabbed him in the back. But he sensed me and moved just enough for me to his heart, then swatted me away like a pain-in-the-ass little brother.

He swore in anger and stormed closer, an all-consuming urge to snap my neck emanating from his face. But as Becca attempted to writhe free from his grasp, his desire to drink her blood was far stronger. Instead of beating me, he turned and took a flying leap right out the fifth-story window, my only child screaming in his grasp.

I cried out, thinking she would be killed by the fall, but he defied gravity and flew up with her into the snow-filled sky. I stuck my head out through the fractured glass and torn screen, thinking he might swoop down and pull me out to my doom. But I glanced up and caught a glimpse of him gliding over the roof. He was going to drain her blood up there. I had to stop him, but I couldn't waste time trying to reach the eighth-floor access door. It was usually locked anyway.

The storm surged with an icy wind that forced me away from the sill, but I fought back, spotting a downspout nearby. It was a stretch, but I just reached it. I slipped on the icy windowsill and grabbed hold, dangling fifty feet above the parking lot. A huge piece of window frame broke loose and plummeted to the concrete, shattering across the drifts.

Scientists may argue that gravity and electromagnetism are some of the most powerful forces in the universe, but on strictly human terms, love and adrenaline are the true miracle workers. My hands gripped the downspout like vises, actually crunching the metal as I climbed. Sheets of thin ice cracked and fell away.

My sock-covered feet found toeholds in the grooves between layers of bricks. I was never so grateful that the homeowners' association had ignored my repeated pleas to repair the tuckpointing. I had to strain my way up three floors. It took a lot longer than I would have liked. My head was spinning, and the ground was dizzying.

Normally, when a parent hears their child scream, that's when they charge in for the rescue. But Becca's screams had stopped, which was ten times more frightening. Was I already too late? Had he drained enough of her blood to stop her precious heart from ever beating again?

I couldn't waste time worrying. If I fell, my life would end. But I couldn't die. I had to save her. Every inch was a struggle. It's not like people practice climbing gutters for fun and profit. Then I heard Becca scream again, and I felt a blood rush of my own. My friends used to tell me that whenever I was in a fight, I went gonzo. They couldn't even get through to me. I was in a different zone. That's what I felt at that moment, for the first time in decades.

I scrambled up that structure like a 190-pound squirrel. My hands bent the gutter, which curled down in my fingers. I kicked up from the frame of the eighth-story window, smashing the glass. It gave me just enough leverage to pull myself over the concrete embankment.

There he was, slurping on her neck, gore everywhere. A father's worst nightmare. Becca looked like she was already dead. I had to stop him immediately, but the long climb had sucked the life from my body.

"Anton!" I screamed, falling to my knees. "You gutless pussy. Picking on little girls. Don't have the guts to fight a man your own size, do ya?"

Anton glared up at me with all the hatred I knew he had always felt for me. Exploding from his crouched position, he skied twenty feet in a split second, walloping me on the forehead with a punch that would have taken my head clean off. I ducked just in time; otherwise, he would have cold cocked my lifeless corpse right over the edge of the roof.

I was down for the count. I think he fractured my skull. He looked down at me with an arrogance that only centuries of surviving as one of the living dead could create. I was helpless, pleading in incoherent mumbles for him to let Becca live. He laughed with a conceit that only a demon could radiate.

Anton could have killed me then and there, but it seemed he wanted to make me watch as he stole every last drop of blood from Becca's veins. This was it. I had mere seconds to stop him before my baby would be his slave forever. I prayed to Dawn in heaven to give me strength. Inch by inch I crawled toward them, then realized I had nothing to kill him with.

That hollow, piercing laugh erupted from his lips one last time as he went in for the kill. I tugged at his pant leg, desperate to save her.

At that moment, my will to live melted away. If I lost Becca to this monster, I would be too tormented and ashamed to bear another day. Then in my morose little bubble, I thought I heard bells. Jingling bells, coming closer and closer, muffled by the dampening snow.

Suddenly, three spikes burst through Anton's chest. His conceited expression transformed into one of shock and despair. He shrieked in pain, his cry echoing hollowly into the night. That look of surprise in his eyes warmed my heart, gave me hope.

The whole thing was so confusing, but somehow he was launched forward, still hanging from the stakes. But they weren't stakes. They were antlers. Reindeer antlers. More appeared from the crystal mist, eight in total, all pulling a sleigh. Their hooves touched down, and they all skidded off to the left, sliding along the roof so they wouldn't bump over the rail.

At the back, sitting in the sleigh, was Santa Claus. Yes, St. Nicholas himself. He wasn't wearing a fluffy, cartoonish outfit like he was in a Rankin/Bass special. He wore red survival gear, the stuff you would need to survive at the harsh North Pole. His hair and beard were pure white, like an abominable snowman, all wild and outdoorsy. The skin on his face was flushed and leathery, as if he'd been living in the frosty wilderness for centuries.

Anton whimpered from his antler perch. If I counted right, it was Dasher who had plucked him away from my daughter. He held firm, the massive muscles in his neck protruding. Santa hopped down from his seat and gazed upon Becca's lifeless form. He bent down and lifted her with one hand as if she were a baby, a glow burning from his glove.

The glow enveloped her, and the blood on her neck receded back into the punctures. He pointed at the dangling vampire, and all the crimson hemoglobin vacuumed from his lips and shot through the air directly into Becca's veins. Then the punctures sealed themselves, healing without scars.

Santa stomped toward me, an adventurer, a Viking, the living embodiment of what a man from the Middle Ages would have looked like. I tried to climb to my knees to thank him, but I fell back in a heap. He leaned down and clutched my shoulder, staring into my eyes with the penetrating gaze of an ancient wizard. New energy swirled inside my body, rejuvenating my soul. My head even stopped bleeding.

Becca soon regained consciousness, as alive as she'd ever been. Santa let her down into my arms. His energy healed all of our injuries.

"Lots of beasties still running around from Halloween," he said in a grim yet sweet tone. "Have to wipe as many off the face of the planet as I can before the new year arrives."

He put one hand on each of us and grinned. "I sense the love you two have for each other is so great, no gifts from me are necessary. But just as I have mended your wounds, I have also filled the holes in your hearts. Merry Christmas."

With that he bounded back onto his sleigh.

"On Dasher. You look like you have an extra delivery to make."

The reindeers' hooves clicked across the roof, and the entire ensemble rose into the sky. Becca and I hugged each other with more emotion than we have had since she was a little girl. As we watched them fly off to make their rounds, we bawled like babies. We stayed like that for a while. Our only movements were the happy little twitches caused by sobs. She felt like my little baby again.

But it was more than that. It felt like part of Dawn was inside her too. Whatever it was, the everlasting spirit or DNA or Santa's yuletide magic, my wife was inside my baby just then—and in my heart. My chest warmed up the way it used to when Dawn and I would cuddle together at night. I could sense her, and she was crying with us too. But they were happy tears. We were all finally back together. Dawn would never be truly apart from us ever again.

In the distance we saw Dasher shake Anton, who was still wriggling, off his antlers. He plummeted toward the ground, screaming as he fell into the smokestack from the garbage disposal plant a few blocks away.

Straight into the incinerator to his death.

We heard mirthful laughter ringing through that magical night.

"Ho-Ho-Hoooooo!"

That Santa really has a thing for chimneys.